APOCALYPSE ALLEY

DON ALLMON

RIPTIDE
PUBLISHING

Riptide Publishing
PO Box 1537
Burnsville, NC 28714
www.riptidepublishing.com

Apocalypse Alley

Cover art: Simoné, dreamarian.com
Editor: Sarah Lyons
Layout: L.C. Chase, lcchase.com/design.htm

ISBN: 978-1-62649-666-8

First edition
February, 2018

Also available in ebook:
ISBN: 978-1-62649-665-1

APOCALYPSE ALLEY

DON ALLMON

RIPTIDE
PUBLISHING

TABLE OF CONTENTS

CHAPTER ONE

Spent casings littered the parking lot. A dead Atari Koroshiya 036 urban combat drone lay drowned in its own hydraulic oils, a twisted, scarred wreck. Scraps of high-tensile netting and plastic shards from burst floodlights sparkled in the afternoon sunlight. There were bullet holes punched in the corrugated walls and divots blasted out of concrete. The whole compound stank of burnt wiring.

It looked like Yingkiong, or Beylagan, or Kampong Cham, or any number of other torn-up places Comet had been deployed to. It didn't look like Arizona. It didn't look like Jason's home.

Comet had known something was wrong the moment he'd stepped off the plane after six months deployed to India and Jason hadn't been there waiting with balloons and a cold welcome-home beer he would party-trick open with one tusk. Comet had needed to cab it to Duke's place. There, he had gone straight for his bike and pistol, hadn't even said hi to Duke.

Duke had seen him leaving and sent, —*Where are you going?* over the net, the Old Man's voice simulated directly into his brain. It sounded like Comet's own thoughts, except different.

—*Something's wrong.* And on the ride to Jason's compound, his cold-gut feeling got worse and worse, and now here was all the evidence of a goddamn war.

He almost signaled his squad. He didn't because they were on holiday now, just like he was, and this was Arizona, not Arunachal Pradesh, and he refused to admit home had changed so badly as that.

—*Raiders hit Jason*, he sent to Duke, glad for once that the sending protocol didn't carry tone well. It kept the hint of panic out of his words.

He slipped off his modded Kawasaki, slaved his 9mm Israeli Qayin, and pressed himself tight against the wall of the nearest shed.

Duke had told Jason not to build so far outside of town: no one to call for help if a raiding band swept through. It was four K to the next home, ten K to Greentown. But Jason had to have his privacy.

Comet linked his vision so Duke could see what he saw. He started recording, standard procedure.

Jason's home and business was a concrete enclosure turreted on each of four corners. It had one entrance: a drive with sunken hydraulic bollards and a gate that was closed and electrified at night. Right now it was open, and the bollards were down. Inside the wall was an open yard of mixed paving and gravel big enough to park five or six cars or APCs or whatever vehicle Jason was printing at the time—empty now, except for Comet's motorcycle and way too many bullet casings.

Six buildings ringed the yard: a toolshed (Comet tight against it), an armory, a storage warehouse, an empty garage (all the doors rolled up so he could see inside), Jason's home (single story, concrete and steel, Bauhaus would have approved), and the printer lab. The printer lab sat catty-corner to the house. It had two doors: a bay door for the vehicles Jason printed, and a standard people-sized door. The bay door was closed. The people-sized door had been blown off its hinges and lay bent against the frame.

None of the other buildings had been messed with, not even the armory, which Comet found curious, because if he'd been the one to raid this place, he'd have cracked that armory wide open. Jason built more than motorcycles and monster trucks.

—*Find survivors*, Duke sent. That word *survivors*, sterile and analytical, steadied Comet, as if it wasn't Jason they were talking about.

Pistol in both hands, Jedi-blue cybernetic eyes flickering through wavelength bands (seeing nothing, seeing nothing, seeing nothing), he leapt up the shed wall, then from one roof to another light as a feather. Grandmaster Natalia Jen had taught him to fly the way the old heroes used to. It was called *qīnggōng*, and he'd almost been a master. He'd nearly lost it all when his cybernetic and genetic modifications permanently disrupted his *qì*. These fantastic leaps were the best he could do anymore.

He landed at the front door of Jason's home and slipped inside.

The AC was busted. The air was acrid but infrared showed no fires. There was no one here. On the dining table lay a pair of open tungsten handcuffs and a half-eaten mustard sandwich. The bread was mostly soft. On impulse, he took the handcuffs, reset the code, and slipped them into his jacket pocket.

He returned to the yard and inspected the ruined combat drone. It had looked something like a mantis, once. It was pitted from high caliber bullets and its hydraulic tubing had been laid bare and cut at several critical points. Across its chest was hand-painted the word: *DOC.* The Atari Koroshiya 036 was expensive. They could work independently on their limited virtual intelligence, but to be worth the cost, they needed a skilled pilot. If there were more than a few hundred skilled pilots in the world, Comet would have been surprised. Pilots like those lived their lives 24/7/52 in deep sleep, their entire interaction with the real world through the drones they controlled. Duke would have given both nuts and also thrown in Comet's to get someone like that on the payroll, and Duke really liked Comet's nuts. They'd cost him a fortune.

Comet checked for the Atari's brain, but the slot was empty. Someone had taken care to remove any evidence of what had happened here.

Through the broken door of the printer building, Comet heard a woman's voice: "Help me, Dante Riggs. You're my only hope."

That was just about the last thing Comet had expected to hear. Dante Riggs was Jason's kid apprentice. Comet had never liked her.

He held his pistol close enough to his cheek he could feel its coolant. He leaned around the bent doorframe of the printer control room and looked in.

There was a man in the room. Comet didn't know who he was, except he didn't belong here.

He was standing amid the tangle of thick power cables that fed a hemispherical bank of eight 210-centimeter monitors behind him and was watching the projection from a large floor holo-display. It was working on backup power and projected a life-sized, staticked-up image of a pickup truck jacked high on immense wheels. The door of the holographic truck opened and a holographic woman dropped down from the cab to the ground. She wore a one-piece dress and her hair was done in an afro. The tips of her ears showed through. She was an elf and she was pretty. All elven women were. She said, "Help me, Dante Riggs. You're my only hope." And then the whole hologram went static and reset to the beginning: truck, door, woman, "Help me, Dante Riggs . . ."

The man didn't look like a raider. Raiders wore body armor and bristled with knives and guns. This guy didn't look to have a single weapon on him. He was as white as white guys got and probably Irish. He looked like a college kid out on spring break: cargo shorts and a flannel shirt over a faded T-shirt, white socks, and the antique kind of sneakers that never went out of style. He hadn't had a haircut in a year and might not have owned a comb. His hair hung to his shoulders in a shaggy mass of loose copper curls and played mischief with his eyes.

He was adorable, and that was a damn shame, because any other time and place and the conversation they were about to have would have been completely different. Comet's targeting laser brushed the guy's cheek and settled over his temple. The guy was so deep in his study of the hologram, he didn't even notice. Comet marked him as an enemy combatant and labeled him "Shaggy" so his gun knew who to kill, then he said, "Move and I'll shoot you."

Shaggy yelped and his hands shot up in surrender. Comet crossed the room fast and smooth, gun arm steady, and the little red dot wavered less than a few centimeters. Comet grabbed him by his shirt and shoved him back until he hit the bank of monitors. Shards of broken plexi clattered down.

He jammed his pistol under Shaggy's jaw. "Where's Jason? Who the fuck are you?"

Shaggy sputtered. Behind them, the hologram looped. "Help me, Dante Riggs. You're my only hope."

Comet lifted him so his feet were dangling. He didn't weigh much. Comet could hold him up left-handed. He pressed the gun in harder. There was gonna be a bruise. The guy's eyes rolled down and went mostly white trying to see the pistol buried in his chin. He said, "Qayin," and closed his eyes like he was waiting to be killed.

Comet felt the smart link drop. The gun shut down. He pulled the trigger out of reflex. Nothing happened. This guy here had just hacked his weapon that fucking fast.

Shaggy took advantage of Comet's surprise, twisted free, and sprinted hard for the door. Comet tackled him effortlessly—the guy wasn't modded—and had him in an arm lock a moment later.

The guy cussed up a storm and huffed and whined as tears sprang into his eyes because that lock hurt, Comet knew. Comet tightened it so it hurt more.

"Now you're gonna answer my questions."

—*Bring him in*, Duke sent, having watched the whole thing through Comet's eyes. *He'll answer mine.*

Comet grinned wickedly. "Now you really fucked up." He snapped the handcuffs on the guy and dragged him back to Greentown to see Duke.

Comet had met Jason three wars ago. Comet kept time by counting wars, so, for the record, three wars was two years. He'd just come back from Cambodia and the Chey Dara debacle, and he'd been feeling ornery, needing to work all the sourness out of him.

The music at 501 Main had been orcabilly, a retro-sounding industrial folk. It had been Saturday-night crowded on a Friday night on account of the game, though nobody watched it.

They wouldn't let orcs play in the IPL anymore, not after Harris had taken a tusk in the gut and left small intestines from the ten to the five. All the orcs were still protesting the ban. Games were just another excuse to go out and get drunk and complain about humans, like there weren't already enough excuses for that. The place was dark (except that one monitor that was showing the game no one was watching). The orcs liked it dark. As a bonus, it kept the human tourists out, though a few came in anyway like it was the ultimate double-dog dare.

As one of Duke's favorites, Comet didn't count as human. Sometimes Comet liked that. Sometimes he didn't. When he got a bit drunk and a bit philosophical, he thought that being human and one of Duke's favorites was a little like being Chinese-Pacificker— belonging to two worlds but fitting in neither. A little like that. That night he hadn't minded being an honorary orc.

"Who's the new guy?" Comet had said. That's what he'd said, not any of the other shit Duke later claimed.

Duke saw the guy Comet meant. He was runty for an orc, which meant he was still bigger than Comet. "You like him?"

"Just never seen him before."

Duke ordered New Guy a drink over BarNet. It appeared at the bottom of the queue. "Aw, Old Man, I was just askin'." But Duke's influence in the town meant Duke's orders didn't wait in queues. It was already gone, and it was too late to complain.

New Guy popped the lid off his beer with one tusk—a cute trick—and tipped it toward Duke mouthing thanks, but the Old Man wasn't letting him off so easy and called him over with a jerk of his head. New Guy looked around like he didn't want to. Comet didn't blame him. Duke made people nervous.

Duke was big—every goddamn thing about him and then some. Duke's tusks were the biggest Comet had ever seen. They were carved like scrimshaw and inlaid with gold. Duke's hair was a steel-gray mane bound up into ropes by a hundred gold rings that took a stylist an hour to thread. His skin was more gray than green. He had a face creased as Wisdom's. And his eyes weren't black; they were a strange gray like orcs never had. Duke dressed like a businessman. His collared white shirts were custom-made. He wore a turquoise bolo tie and cuff links made from human molars. Duke had pulled them himself, but he wouldn't tell anyone who they'd belonged to. He said it was between him and that man. He said it like that man was still alive, just missing some teeth.

Comet had been a security contractor with Duke's company, Irontooth Enterprises, for four wars (just over two years) at the time. He wasn't the captain of Reindeer Squad yet, but everyone already knew he would be. Local talk said Duke was grooming Comet to take over the company when the Old Man died. Comet could barely imagine that. The "Old Man" was only fifty. He'd survived the Awakening (and the stories of his transformation into an orc were terrifying and sad the way most of those stories were), and he'd survived all the shit since, and nothing would kill him short of a meteor to the head.

New Guy didn't find a good excuse to stay away, so he came on over.

Duke's idea of introduction went like this: "My boy here thinks you're hot."

"That's not what I said," Comet said.

"Ah. No. What my boy said was, 'That orc there would look better with my cock down his throat.'"

Comet's shoulders, neck, and face went red. It was true now that Duke had pointed it out. New Guy had a mouth made for fucking: broad, full lips that had to be soft, tusks not so big or sharp you'd worry too much about things going wrong, just big enough to add the thrill Comet liked. Comet looked away and mumbled at the tabletop, "That's not what I said."

"Ah. No. What my boy said was, 'That orc there would look better with my jizz dripping down his ass.'"

Comet went deeper red, so red it hurt like his cheeks were gonna bust. He shook his head and laughed because he couldn't help it. What was New Guy thinking? Did he think this was funny? Was he getting pissed off? Most guys got pissed off. It was an asshole-ish kind of game Duke liked to play. But Comet couldn't meet New Guy's eyes he was so damn embarrassed.

"Ah. No. What my boy said was—"

Duke would do this all night if Comet didn't stop him. "What I said was, 'Who's the new guy?'" Comet looked up.

New Guy didn't seem pissed. New Guy seemed like he didn't know what to think. New Guy's cheeks and ears had gone dark, embarrassment flaring. In better light, the color would have been that of leaves turning autumn red. Comet tried not to glance at New Guy's crotch, but did anyway because how could he not, and he was pretty sure this orc was packing something big.

Duke said, "Oh, that's right. I remember now. That's what you said. 'Who's the new guy?' Hah! What was I thinking?" He stretched his enormous arms along the seat back, lounged, and smiled, gleefully pleased with the way he'd embarrassed everyone. "Have a seat."

Duke's booth was a corner booth with a semicircle bench. New Guy slid in opposite Duke, next to Comet. Not too close.

He was wearing a red baseball cap with a stitched-on label: three inverted triangles and the letters *MF*. Comet didn't know what that meant and had to look it up. "You a farmer?" He kind of hoped he was, because Comet had never fucked a farmer before (never even met one), and everyone knew farmers were filthy as hell.

"No. I just like the hat. You a cowboy?"

Comet was dressed as trashy as could be. He wore a Christian Texas-sized turquoise belt buckle because it was gaudy and made people stare at his crotch, a threadbare tank top that showed his shoulders off, and a faux-straw cowboy hat that had been crushed beneath fucking bodies so often it glowed under black light and Luminol.

Comet broke out his dirtiest, sly grin. "I'm a kind of cowboy."

"What kind is that?"

"The break-him-before-I-ride-him kind." This banter here, it was all make believe and didn't mean nothing. Comet could do it without going red. Duke's teasing was different somehow. No matter how close they'd grown in only four wars, he was always afraid Duke's teasing was for real.

"That so?" New Guy said. "What if he's already broken?"

"There's always something left to break. Just gotta know where to look. Sometimes looking's the fun part."

They tried to hold each other's eyes with a serious stare. This was supposed to be hot, not funny. They both raised their beers to hide breaking grins. They both waited a moment before drinking so they didn't choke on a laugh and blow beer out their noses.

Duke laughed. Everyone in the bar turned to see. Duke's laughs were like thunder. "Ain't that adorable! The two of you embarrassed."

"I ain't—" both New Guy and Comet said at the same time. They stopped at the same time.

Duke thought that was even funnier. His laughter boomed and rumbled all over. "I'm gonna love watching the two of you fuck."

Good sign: New Guy didn't run when Duke said that. Plenty of sensible guys did. Duke and Comet weren't lovers and never had been. But Duke liked to watch and Comet liked to show off.

"What's your name?" Comet said.

"Jason Taylor."

"Comet."

"On account of the hair?" Comet's hair was nano-dyed flame colors. It was temperature sensitive and heat made it flicker.

"On account of I'm me. Welcome to Greentown, Jason Taylor. I'll be your top tonight."

CHAPTER TWO

Buzz Howdy made a scene, hoping someone would save him. He shouted, "You can't do this! You're not the police! I ain't done nothing wrong!" Which wasn't quite true. He was a hacker, a forger, and a thief, and had done plenty wrong—just not today.

He fought the crazy gene-job fucker who had him by the scruff of his shirt and was pushing him around, and tried to make sure everyone in the dark bar could see he'd been handcuffed.

But this wasn't Pacifica. This was an anarchist town in Freestate Arizona, and there weren't no police.

All those orcs looked at him, then looked at the guy holding him, then turned back to their small knots of friends gathered around tables, talking low or talking loud, making deals or promises or just shooting the shit like there wasn't a little red-headed human in the middle of their bar about to get the hell beaten out of him. Probably the crazy fucker could have whacked him right here in front of everyone, and no one would have said a goddamn word except to complain about the splatter.

"Got anything else you want to tell everyone?" the fucker growled in his ear.

Buzz knew plenty of guys like him. He could have gotten eyes that looked natural, but instead had replaced them with one of the solid glow models to ramp up the cool factor (and so he'd picked Jedi blue instead of Sith red, what difference did that matter?), a genetically engineered porn-star body, and a violent streak looking for every opportunity to show it off. He bet the guy had a three-decimeter dick and thought it was something special, like anyone couldn't have one for twenty grand. Buzz would have spit at him if he'd ever learned how to spit, but he hadn't, so he said, "Fuck off," instead.

He wrenched Buzz over to a corner table. The table had a two-meter DMZ around it where no one else stood. Seated there was the biggest orc Buzz had ever seen. Buzz knew Duke Mason by sight.

And apparently Duke knew him. "Buzz Howdy. You know who you've found, Comet? This here is Buzz Howdy, dumbest hacker on the planet. Have a seat, Buzz."

Comet—yeah, he'd have to be named something like Comet, wouldn't he?—shoved him into the booth and then slid in after him so Buzz couldn't get out.

—*He's right. This is dumb. You shouldn't be here.* A teenage boy flipped the cap of an ancient lighter and lit an ancient cigarette. Orcs passed through him like he wasn't there because he wasn't. He was an illusion, the consequence of stimuli injected into Buzz's head, which meant no one could see him or hear him but Buzz. His name was BangBang. He looked like a fourteen-year-old James Dean. Buzz had never heard of James Dean and had refused to look it up, so BangBang'd had to tell him, and now he held a friendly grudge about it.

On BangBang's shoulder sat a mouse named Critter. Critter wasn't really a mouse. The two of them belonged to the 3djinn "data liberation" consortium, like Buzz. Unlike Buzz, they were two of the 3.

BangBang spun an illusionary chair around, sat, and crossed his arms over the chair's back. Illusionary lips synced perfectly: —*Do you know who that is? That's Duke Mason. He's dangerous. He's like a whole fucking rogue nation all stuffed into one orc. He's caused more wars than we have.*

—*I know who Duke Mason is.*

Duke was the sole owner and CEO of Irontooth Enterprises, not the largest private military company in the world—Duke could only field around 7,000 security contractors—but one of the most high-profile. Their logo could be seen in the background of nearly every high-level politico on the planet, sewn onto the sleeves of their security detail. He had direct lines to senators, generals, and cabinet members worldwide. And he'd set up shop in Greentown, not for any egalitarian dream, but because Arizona was a freestate and not a signatory to the UN resolutions that governed PMCs. So no, he wasn't a criminal, but only by virtue of living in a place where the laws were decided by those with the biggest guns.

Comet dropped his pistol on the table with a heavy *clunk*. He turned it so it was pointed Buzz's way like they were playing spin the bottle and it was Buzz's turn.

The gun was still lifeless. Buzz sneered at him. "Ain't all that dumb, am I?"

Comet drew his hand back for a good slap.

Buzz flinched and glared. He said to Duke, "Your merc here—"

"I'm a PMC, not a merc."

"—ignored a zero-day patch on his gun. You'd think a competent P-M-C would keep his gun up-to-date."

Duke's eyes narrowed, and Comet looked down at the table. "I've been fourteen hours on a plane. My weapon was stowed."

—You were supposed to be going into hiding, coming to High Castle to be with us, BangBang sent.

—I'm not here by choice. Can you not feel the handcuffs? BangBang was a rider. He had full access to Buzz's sensoria when he wanted. It was how he was able to manifest the illusion of himself so perfectly. And the handcuffs pinched and held Buzz's arms at a bad angle so they'd gone sore and a bit numb and tingly. There was no way BangBang could have not known if he was paying any attention.

"Fix your goddamn pistol," Duke said to Comet. He pointed at Buzz. "You. Shut the fuck up."

The whole table fell silent. Duke's and Comet's eyes went mid-distance stare: the sign that their attention was now focused on a cyberspace Buzz couldn't see.

—Can you access their space? Buzz asked BangBang.

The teenage James Dean shook his head. *—Irontooth. Not even gonna try.* Maybe BangBang had tried hacking Mason's company once upon a time and it hadn't gone so well.

No one spoke. Buzz sat and fidgeted.

Comet's hands moved over his pistol, resetting it by sheer muscle memory.

Comet's hands were all tendon and bone. The tone of his skin made his thick roadmap veins appear green. And they weren't scarred up at all, not like Buzz thought a fighter's hands should be scarred. No calluses, nothing. Those hands were deadly strong, Buzz already knew, but the way they brushed over his gun didn't seem deadly at all. Buzz could almost forget it was a gun he was touching that way.

The gun's lights came on. Buzz could have hacked it again before the patch was complete, but what was the point? (Except to watch those hands reset it again?)

Minutes passed. Duke's and Comet's eyes shifted focus from time to time. Buzz felt ignored. And after a few more minutes of being ignored, he felt a bit forgotten.

BangBang sent, —*I've hacked the BarNet. I'll wipe all the customer accounts and that will give you time to slip away.*

—*No! I ain't slipping away.*

—*After you double-crossed the Electric Dragon Triad, it was a lot of work getting you to safety—*

—*It was a lot of work for JT and Austin, not you.*

—*And what you're doing right now undoes all of it.*

—*Right now, JT is in trouble. Someone attacked him. I want to know who and why, and then I'm going to do something about it. He's my friend.*

—*I'm your friend.*

—*You're not in danger.*

"I could help," Buzz said aloud.

—*You're wrong, Buzz. I am in danger. And you know who's putting me in danger? You.*

"Oh really? You could help?" Duke said. "Go ahead, then. Help me."

Their eyes didn't focus on him. They expected him to lie, so he didn't. Except this one: These people would only know JT by the fake identity Buzz had created for him. They called him Jason Taylor. Buzz had to remember to call him that too.

"I followed an AI fragment to Jason's place. It's called the Blue Unicorn. That holo recording you saw when you found me, that was it. A recording of it, at least. By the time I got there, the place was shot up. Jason and Austin—Austin's an old friend of Jason's, a way-back kind of friend, they were together the last time I saw them—they were both missing. Dante too, I guess."

The whole thing had been terrifying. He'd searched everywhere for the three of them and each room and building he'd entered, he'd been certain he'd find his friends dead. He squirmed in the seat, the handcuffs biting. "I was searching the place's security records when your asshole showed up. I didn't find anything. There'd been a cyberattack and the whole network was a wreck."

"Why would an AI fragment ask for Dante?" Comet said.

Buzz shrugged and shook his head. He didn't know.

"Why did it go to Jason's place?"

"I don't know."

"Who shot up the place? The AI didn't do that."

"I don't know."

"Where's Jason?"

"I don't know."

"Is he okay? Is he hurt? Is he captured? Is he dead?"

"I don't know!"

"So you're useless. Or a liar. Or both. Thanks for the fucking help."

"I'm not lying!"

Comet didn't let up with the questions. "Did you take the hard drive out of that Atari?"

"You frisked me. Did you find it?"

"Answer the question," Duke said.

"It was already gone when I got there. I told you, someone cleaned the place up data-wise. There was nothing left."

Duke set a holo puck in the center of the table. Comet protested. "You're trusting him?"

The puck activated and projected an image of the wrecked yard of JT's compound. It was 3-D, probably created from video recorded by Comet's cybernetic eyes. The image shrank until it showed the whole yard in shimmering green. Some places had been highlighted and glowed a brighter green. Duke moved from one highlighted space to the next: long gouges in the pavement, punctures through corrugated siding that didn't look like bullet holes, pieces of twisted metal.

Duke said, "Comet's run an analysis of the battlefield—"

Buzz blinked at the word *battlefield*, and he saw Comet's jaw clench. Comet didn't like JT's place being called a battlefield any more than he did. Maybe they had something in common after all.

"—and from the damage, tracks, and debris, he's confident there were *three* Atari Koroshiya 036s. Though I can't imagine how Jason might have done it, he managed to disable one of the three."

He gave Buzz the opportunity to explain how a mild-mannered engineer like JT could have held his own against three high-end urban combat drones long enough to take one out.

The answer was that JT wasn't a mild-mannered engineer. But Buzz said nothing.

The image focused on the dead Atari drone. Duke blew the image up until its chest filled the puck's projection area. Centered there was the word *DOC* painted in childlike sloppy tempera.

"Mean anything to you?" Duke asked.

Buzz studied it. He'd noticed the word at the time, of course, but hadn't thought much of it. All his attention had been on data recovery; the idea that there might be something else worth investigating hadn't occurred to him. But now that he saw it, there was something familiar.

He accessed a 3djinn database of images and video stolen from top-secret files worldwide. He felt BangBang and Critter looking over his shoulder. Critter began to chatter, and BangBang cussed. He found images of wreckage just like that Atari, with names painted on them in comic tempera. All those images were connected to one person.

"Valentine," he said.

Duke sighed, sat back, and crossed his arms. Probably he didn't trust a direct sending link with Buzz, because he requested a secure anonymous drop, and then shared an encrypted folder with both Comet and Buzz (and though Duke didn't know it, by extension BangBang and Critter). Buzz opened it. The folder contained PBI and Interpol reports on a cybernetically enhanced drone pilot and assassin code-named Valentine. She'd been credited with a dozen high-profile murders, including the British Prime Minister Beau Geddings (Bright-Green Party) and the orc mystic Odoro Hazzell. She had warrants for her arrest in almost every country and extradition agreements between all the North American unions, the

Commonwealth, the EU, the Caliphate, Egypt, and even China, who never agreed to extradition with anyone.

"So a world-class assassin and a 3djinn hacker followed an AI fragment to Jason's house, where they found it asking for help from a teenage orc."

Buzz shook his head slowly. Because when put that way, it did seem unbelievable. Had he and JT and Austin fucked up so badly by getting involved with the Blue Unicorn that someone had sent Valentine after them?

He should run. He should go into hiding and never come out. And like he was reading Buzz's mind, BangBang sent, —*Hide, Buzz. Take the* Marid *and come to High Castle with us like you said you were going to, and hide.*

It was the sensible thing to do. Take 3djinn's stolen spaceship and get as far away from Greentown as he could. Because if that assassin had come for JT and Austin, she'd come for him too, wouldn't she?

Maybe Duke was right and he was the dumbest hacker on the planet, because he didn't tell BangBang yes. What he said was: "You said there were three? Two other Ataris? They'll have recorded the fight and everything that happened before I got there, right? Probably other data too? We grab one of her drones and we get our answers."

"And how am I supposed to find her?" Comet said.

—*You've lost your goddamn mind,* BangBang sent.

"We set a trap. She came after the Blue Unicorn. So we blast that we've found the Blue Unicorn over the net, all nodes, and Valentine will come to us. You distract her. I hack a drone. We find Jason."

—*You don't stand a chance, Buzz!*

—*Then help me!*

—*I'm not going to threaten our network to help your idiot friends. It's not just you you're putting at risk. It's the whole 3djinn network. You know passwords—*

—*So change them!*

—*and encryption algorithms and you know the identities of contacts and clients.*

"I'll do it," Comet said and slid out of the seat.

"Great." Buzz turned so Comet could remove the cuffs.

"You ain't going nowhere." Comet said.

—and if Valentine gets into your head—

"You're taking him with you," Duke said.

—It's all of 3djinn at risk!

—Either help me or get the fuck out of my head!

"I don't want him with me."

"You need a hacker."

"I need a hacker I trust. I'll call Prancer."

"Prancer's four hours out in Mexico City. Take him with you, and find JT and Dante and this friend of his, Austin, and bring them back safe. That's your mission, Comet."

BangBang and Critter went quiet and icy and then vanished.

Comet didn't like Duke's orders one bit, Buzz could tell. Comet rolled his shoulders. A coiling-snake-strike crouching-panther-like sort of movement, patiently vicious. His whole body rippled with the strength of it. It was arrogant (and Buzz disliked the guy just that much more), intimidating, and entirely, unhealthily, confusingly thrilling.

Comet hauled Buzz out of the booth and turned him around. As he undid the cuffs, he leaned in close and whispered in Buzz's ear, "You're still my prisoner."

Comet pocketed the cuffs and went for the door. Buzz went to follow, but Duke's immense hand closed around his arm. "One more thing, 3djinn."

Buzz tried to pull away, but Duke's grip was iron. He scowled at Comet near the door and refused to look back at Duke.

"Before I dumped forty million into Jason's start-up car shop, I did my research. Jason Taylor was a kid from nowhere Montana who just barely got himself accepted to Hyundai-Daisho Davis. Bs in his coursework. Second-string on the Halo team. Capstone paper on the shear-strength of nano-engineered plasti-ceramics—boring as shit if you ask me. Doubly so considering the same paper was written by another student two years previous at Cornell. Jason's indenture to HD was ten years. He gave them four and skipped out on the last six. No record how he paid off the other quarter million he owed them for his education."

Buzz looked over his shoulder at the orc. "So Jason's got debt problems. Who doesn't?"

"That's my point, ain't it? No one's an angel. Everyone's in debt. So the summary on that report I got, it says here's a kid who was so goddamn average no one would look at him twice. A kid who cheated when it was easy, and toed the line when it wasn't, just like every other kid ever did."

"So why'd you invest?"

"I had a hunch. That was two years ago, and me and Comet here, we've spent a lot of time with Jason, and we've grown close, I like to think. And here's the Jason I know: He's a genius. He understands engines and metals and plastics like nobody does. And he's driven. He's driven like no twentysomething I've ever seen except maybe Comet. Everyday twentysomethings don't start their own businesses. They don't chase after defense contracts. Jason Taylor isn't second-string anything."

Duke let go of him. Buzz's arm went pins and needles when the blood started pumping back into it. Duke lounged back in his seat, shrewd eyes narrow. "So all that background I dug up? I don't believe one bit of it. That background was forged by you, wasn't it? Who is Jason Taylor, really?"

Buzz Howdy wasn't much of a liar. All of his lies were told with code and data and he'd never had to learn how to do it, real-life, face-to-face. It was why he didn't try to cover his own identity. "I don't know what you're talking about. Jason's just Jason." And maybe that was a lie, but he didn't care if Duke believed him or not.

Duke held Buzz's gaze for a good ten seconds, until Buzz couldn't take it anymore and looked away. Anyone would have.

Duke said, "Comet, if this guy crosses you . . ." and then he only shrugged as if the rest was obvious.

This was a party neighborhood: bars, restaurants, smoke, and coffee houses; piercing, tattoo, and scarring parlors; sex shops and sim dens; and even on a weekday the streets were crowded. The traffic was unmanaged the way freestate towns tended to be—windshield-scroll slogans read *DRIVING = FREEDOM* and *MY CAR'S NOT YOUR DRONE*—so there was the stop and go flares of brake lights and piercing horns. Add to that noise the unending chatter of adverts flowing over shop windows, every piece of glass flickering (and none of those models or actors were orcs, except for the beer and the PacArmy commercials, go figure).

Buzz caught up with Comet, who kept a fast pace. People on the street nodded at him as he passed. Everyone seemed to know who he was. "Where we going?"

"To find someplace where people ain't gonna get hurt."

Buzz felt a bit bad for not having thought of that. He took out a joint and lit it. Comet gave him a disapproving look. "We're going into a combat situation."

"I'm nervous, okay?"

"Then maybe you should have stayed behind."

Buzz crushed it out. Comet threaded the crowd fast, and Buzz had to jog a step or two to keep up.

"You want me to send the message now?" The message was simple. Buzz would use the Rainbow Protocol to access the darknets. There were boards in the Ultraviolet network carrying news that people like Valentine would continually scan via virtual intelligences, news of the illegal sort. He'd make a simple post there: GPS coordinates and two words: *Blue Unicorn*. And then they'd wait for someone—likely Valentine—to take the bait.

"Not until we're in position," Comet said.

They stopped at a crosswalk and waited for the signal. It seemed a silly thing to do—the two of them waiting at a crosswalk—all things considered.

Behind them came screams and the shrieking of wheels on pavement. Buzz spun.

Cars stopped, drivers gawked, and the crowd parted to make way for the thing that had dropped from a rooftop onto the sidewalk.

It was mantis-like. One arm was a Swiss Army knife of blades; the other, a gun. Hydraulic tubing glowed red through the seams of armored plating like they were arteries pulsing with irradiated blood. It was the same kind of drone they'd found dead and brainless in the lot of JT's compound. Targeting lasers spun and danced from it like it was a disco ball.

People reacted stupidly. Initial scare over, they laughed because this was Greentown and this kind of thing didn't happen here. It must be some kind of prank, especially because painted in tempera across the robot mantis's chest was the word *COWBOY*.

"I told you not to send the message yet!"

"I didn't!"

"Then why's that thing here?"

All COWBOY's dancing targeting lasers gathered on Buzz.

Buzz and COWBOY stood across from one another just like that: like two gunfighters facing off across the dark oil-in-water-gleaming street of Greentown. The whole street got real quiet like they were supposed to do right before the clock struck high noon.

From a speaker somewhere within the thing came a woman's voice, "I found you, Buzz."

"Run," Comet said.

Buzz couldn't run. He just stood there staring at it, frozen in place as if pinned by all those lasers. The drone didn't shoot him. It charged.

"I said *run*!" Comet shoved him so hard he nearly fell. But he finally ran.

Comet tried to intercept the drone, but COWBOY flung one arm out and knocked him to the street as it raced past. Comet was everywhere near as fast and agile as the drone. He leapt after it and tackled it by its rear legs, and they both tumbled across blacktop—the drone leaving telltale gouges behind it—and slammed up into the fender of a stopped car, crushing it. The driver bailed from the other side.

Comet untangled himself from the drone. Around him: bedlam. People who'd *ooh*ed and *ahh*ed at first, finally realized this wasn't a joke. Some people ran. More drew weapons. They were orcs, after all, and their fight-or-flight instincts were seriously broken. Comet told them, "Stop, stop, *stop*!" but they wouldn't listen. They opened fire on COWBOY.

And then a swerving car clipped him, and Comet flew five meters into the crowd, fall broken by bystanders. He struggled to standing, and shook his head clear, superman body bruised but not broken.

Buzz was long gone. COWBOY too.

Comet cursed himself for not injecting the guy right away with a tracker or setting up a local network between them. He took one-two-three great leaps up windows and fire escapes. He ran rooftop to rooftop, following the damage the drone had left behind, hoping he wasn't too late.

Buzz tore out of there. He bulldozed through orcs. He ran into the street. A car's wheels screeched, a horn blew, and a driver bellowed at him. Behind him: screaming and gunshots. Buzz kept running, not wanting to see the massacre, hoping to God he was wrong and all that screaming was just nerves and not people dying because of him.

BangBang had been right. Buzz shouldn't be here. He ran and blasted BangBang's name all over the local net, hoping he was listening.

He switched from PedX to Rainbow Protocol and accessed the darknets—Black & Blue, Indigo, and Ultraviolet networks—and spent several thousand cryptix on dubious backdoors, vulnerabilities, and exploits for an 036 just in case he had the opportunity to use them.

He leapt trash bins, tripped over others because what was he, some kind of athlete? He jumped for a fire escape ladder, but it was raised and he was short. They made the goddamn things for giants and called it safety. He sprawled flat on the pavement, and just where his head would have been had he not fallen, bolos cracked into prefab. Livewires snapped taut around nothing. COWBOY had found him and wasn't trying to kill him; it was trying to catch him. And being caught by this thing—that scared Buzz shitless.

On your feet again. Ignore the pain in your knees and your palms from falling. Ignore the pain in your side from running and being so damn out of shape. Ignore you can't breathe. Not breathing is better than what that thing'll do. Down one alley, across another. *Fuck it, fuck it if somebody sees,* and he called the *Marid,* sent coordinates and vector. If he brought 3djinn's spaceship down in the middle of Greentown, then that's what he did, and he'd deal with their pissed-off-ness alive instead of dead.

No reply.

He'd taken his ship. BangBang had taken his ship. Buzz flooded the network with an all-nodes string of profanity tagged with BangBang's name.

A second mantis stepped into the alley ahead of him. It had BANDIT painted on its chest. The *N* was backward. COWBOY and BANDIT. It might have been funny.

He juked right. The streets were deserted here, a bad place for walking at night and about to get worse. COWBOY stepped out, spun up its gun, and sprayed bullets down the street in front of Buzz, throwing asphalt everywhere. Buzz skidded to a stop, scrambled away, ducked behind parked cars, lamp posts, a mailbox, anything he could find. Bullets pinged and cracked and whined around him. And then BANDIT appeared in front of him.

Pinned between them, Buzz took his only way out—a narrow alley—knowing this was a trap. They were herding him, but what choice did he have?

He entered the alley hesitantly, skittered around, clung to the cool cinderblock walls, danced one way and then the other, unable to choose between the killer robots or the threat waiting down the dark alley. His pulse raced. His breathing had gone so fast and shallow, he saw spots and thought he'd pass out.

COWBOY and BANDIT came down the alley behind him. Side by side with the blue fade of LED streetlamps behind them, red limning their multi-jointed legs, they looked more insectile than ever, more like something from a B horror sci-fi. The other end of the alley was open, but that was a lie. A trap. Overwhelmed with fear of the drones, he ran anyway.

He made it ten feet.

Framed in the alleyway, the woman who blocked his path was tall and skeletally thin. She was wearing a wide-brimmed bush hat and a brown duster that spread broad like there was a wind. She had one artificial eye big and round as a golf ball, Sith red. She smiled with pointed titanium teeth. She was cybernetic evil like you couldn't buy off the shelf. Valentine.

Buzz took a step back.

A step back into the arms of COWBOY. All six of them snapped closed around him. Neck, chest, waist, thighs, knees, and ankles.

No legs to stand on, all of them around Buzz, the drone plopped onto the pavement, taking Buzz with it. Buzz tried to squirm away. Valentine said, "COWBOY can grind you into hamburger. No, finer than hamburger. Spreadable. Braunschweiger." And, as promised, the arms tightened painfully. Every breath hurt.

The cyborg knelt in front of Buzz. "Your friend got hit by a car back there. I doubt he'll be moving anytime soon."

She's lying, he thought. *That can't be true. He's coming.*

She took a patch cable from her coat.

"What's that for?" His voice was a tight hiss, and he'd started to see spots.

"My employer, Firelight, wants you dead. He wants everyone who came in contact with the Blue Unicorn dead. Even that girl, Dante. But Firelight's a wizard, and wizards don't have a very good grasp of what's valuable and what isn't."

She flipped back long curly hair that belonged on a runway model, not on a nightmare, and snapped the cable into a jack behind her ear. She ruffled her hand through Buzz's shaggy hair. Buzz tried to turn his head away, but he could barely move, and the articulated leg around his throat tightened.

"I saw you at JT's place—you can hide cameras on flies these days—and I know who you are. And when it comes right down to it, the mind of a 3djinn hacker is worth more than any contract Firelight could imagine."

The cyborg found Buzz's jack—these days only a backup connection for when wi-fi wasn't functioning—and went to snap in the cord.

"I'm locked down; you can't get anything."

"You're going to let me in."

"No, I'm not."

Somewhere behind her metal teeth she'd installed LEDs so the red bled through her smile. The corner of her one real eye crinkled up with laugh lines.

"You know who I am. Imagine the things I know, what plots and secrets. Secrets 3djinn could leverage if you're good enough to pry them from my mind. Open up, Buzz. Best hacker wins."

And this was what he'd wanted, wasn't it? Well, not quite this. He'd imagined hacking a half-dead Atari in the safety of a garage somewhere, not this. But it was a solution, wasn't it? And Comet was coming, wasn't he? The idea of being saved by that fucker, of having to listen to his bloated ego, well, that rankled a bit, but he'd suck it up if he had to.

He closed his eyes so the cyborg didn't distract him, and he started building.

BangBang's presence brushed against him. *Thank God. Finally.* He undid his blocks and let him in.

—*Help me.*

—*We warned you.* BangBang ran a quick scan of Buzz. —*What are you doing?* Because Buzz's head was a snowstorm of code flying everywhere, accreting and twisting into spires and loops.

—*Building defenses. I'm going to let her in.*

—*Are you nuts?*

—*She knows what's going on. She knows what happened to JT and Dante because she's the one who did it. If it's data she wants, I'll give her data. If she's downloading, she's open.*

—*You're going to duel her? You've never dueled anyone. You'll lose!*

—*Then help me!*

—*I'm not compromising our network security to help your stupid friends!*

Buzz opened his eyes and fixed on hers. *He's right, this is a stupid idea.* Aloud, he said, "You win, I'm open."

She snapped the cable into place. The sound of its click was a dull vibration traversing bone rather than air, then the cyborg invaded his mind.

CHAPTER THREE

The brain made a slow computer. All its power was in its architecture. Neural implants, heavily based on DNA and peptide computing, were, on a fundamental level, data represented as structure, translated into sensation. Cyberspace wars were geographical, topographical, architectural, like Escherian artists trying to outdraw one another.

Buzz's data stores were palaces of marble, crazed and unhinged, brilliantly out of balance and impossible to navigate by anyone but him. He sank into it, folded hallways and galleries around him, submerged himself beneath the sea of his own consciousness. There was a recursive logic that said you couldn't do that. The THC in his blood made this easier. Other drugs would have made it easier yet, but he'd always been afraid of the side effects. He didn't think Valentine would share those fears. She'd have every edge in this fight.

The cyborg cut loose with a virus Buzz's user interface represented as wisteria. The vines erupted everywhere. They were third-generation meningitis, meant to burn him down, meant to distract him from the real attack by the sheer horror of what they could do to him if left alone. Buzz didn't leave them alone. His honeypots—beautiful Möbius rings of gold—folded around them, trapped them in an infinite fractal space, finitely bounded, and deleted them harmlessly.

In response, he mapped the cyborg's network, building crystalline patterns charting data transfers, which seemed a tepid move by comparison. He mapped the network to COWBOY and BANDIT, analyzed their control paths. Valentine thought he wanted what she knew: details of her assassinations over the years, who paid for them, her contacts. He didn't give a fuck about any of that. The drones had the information he wanted.

He released an army of virtual intelligences, viral bots, to make havoc, knowing the cyborg would squash them flat. What she should have done was let them run.

She was flashy. She wasted bandwidth and processing inserting an image of herself into Buzz's mind: flames jetting from her fingers, Sith eye shooting lasers. It looked badass; it was all bullshit smoke and mirrors, all logic and math constructions, and Buzz reduced all of it down to quadratics and tensor transformations and undid them.

The space in which they fought was like a funhouse hall of mirrors. Real data in its twisting cyclopean spires were hidden behind illusions and then multiplied, bent, and warped so that attacks found nothing. She was impressed. She cackled gleefully. "Now this is what I'm talking about!" and spewed lightning from her fingertips to shatter stained glass windows in Buzz's mind. They fought over the falling shards to build from them chutes and ladders.

Buzz gave ground before her attacks. He played to her vanity (and she was a fuck-ton of vain), so he had to let her burn through data. She burned fast, melting and shattering his virtual mirrors, exposing real data. Buzz couldn't create fictions fast enough. She was relentless and he never had time for a counterstrike.

He started to wonder if he was over his head.

Critter chattered away like some particularly hateful sportscaster calling a football game from another room, all tone and no words. BangBang sent, —*Buzz you need to stop. There's critical data in those structures!*

Buzz's mind contained passwords to databases planetwide. It contained hundreds of thousands of bank accounts, SIN accounts, credit reports, corporate balance sheets, and more. It contained detailed analyses of political money trails, investments, and communications. It contained the intelligence data equivalent to a small country and had access to more.

One structure cracked and folded in a non-Euclidean eye-bending way, breaking before the cyborg's attack and reforming again, damaged and burning. Buzz "forgot" ten thousand IRA accounts just like that.

Critter's complaining didn't stop.

Buzz didn't stop either. JT's, Austin's, and Dante's names hung there in his consciousness, reminders of who he was fighting for. *"He wants everyone who came in contact with the Blue Unicorn dead,"* she'd said.

BangBang sent, — *Your body is our network's greatest vulnerability. You should have lain safe here with us in High Castle, sleeping where no one could touch you. I'm sorry, Buzz. I didn't want to do this. I'm going to shut you down.*

Shutting him down, like he was nothing more than a faulty machine. The words almost didn't register.

Neural implants suffered mechanical failure same as any other system. They could overheat; there were chemical breakdowns; there were viruses. At some level of safety tolerance, a damaged implant would trigger a fail-safe that dropped the wearer into a barbiturate coma to protect the brain from collateral damage. Recovery rates from catastrophic failure without this protection averaged around 6%. With it, 19%.

Buzz's implants were not failing. BangBang was going to send a false-positive and trigger the coma. He was going to drop Buzz into a coma just to save his fucking data.

He threw everything he had at BangBang. He bent BangBang's fucking world into knots even as he realized it was all over now. He couldn't fight Valentine and BangBang both. The cyborg found part of Buzz's porn collection, and it should have been funny she'd waste time burning that, but it wasn't funny. It was a fucking kick in the nuts.

And several levels of consciousness away, his sensation of the external world so dim, fighting a war on two fronts, he almost missed the crack of shots. He felt the equivalent of BangBang and the cyborg both startle: a stuttering in their signals. Gunshots and the physical world filtered in like a dream.

Comet. Thank God. My fucking hero.

Comet's body did all the things it was programmed to do, released all the chems Duke had specced, and his mind went awash with a dreamlike lucidity. He crossed rooftops in two or three bounds.

He crossed alleys and streets in single leaps, chasing the sound of gunshots and a ragged trail of gouges in asphalt and scars on concrete.

And then he found them.

One Atari held Shaggy in a death grip. The second stood guard. And bent over Shaggy, one hand wrapped through his hair, was someone with way too much sense of dramatic evil to be real.

Comet fired on the fucker.

A shot hit the cyborg in the temple with a good solid *whang* and the cyborg's head snapped back. Her hat went spinning, and she dropped to the pavement. Analysis said she wasn't dead. He fired on the drone holding Shaggy, and Shaggy shouted, hoarse and barely audible but for Comet's hearing, "Not that one."

"Not that one"? That's the one that's going to tear him apart! But he switched targets anyway, and the rest of his shots hammered into BANDIT's nano-ceramic plating.

Magazine empty, no spares, he holstered his pistol and raced down the alley. BANDIT, seriously dented but still operational, stepped out and spun up its gun. Comet slid to one side and the bullets flew past. Hand-to-hand now, he pushed the drone's gun away while he tore into the thing with a precision jab. He'd fought these before; he knew their weak spots where critical wiring or hydraulics were located. Its pilot wounded, BANDIT should have been running on native VI, and native VI didn't stand a chance against anyone well trained and Comet was a fuck-ton of well trained. He'd disable it good and fast before the cyborg recovered.

Except the drone twisted and dodged away from Comet's jab and none of his blows connected or slid past its defenses. Knife-bladed insectile limbs deflected him. It rose up on two legs and now it had four limbs to fight with. It flashed knives around. It spun and lashed out. Comet caught its blows on the armored sleeve of his motorcycle jacket. Puffs of pulverized plating and fabric filled the air. Their arms blurred in strike, feint, and counterstrike, beats like a jazz drum solo played too fast.

This shouldn't have happened. He should have taken the drone easily.

Comet leapt away. He crouched low and balanced, hands up and ready, fingers gently curled. The alley went quiet.

The cyborg was already standing. Synthetic skin had been blasted from her forehead, exposing divot-ed metal underneath. A patch cable ran from her head to Shaggy's. Her red eye flickered beneath L'Oréal hair, then steadied.

Comet rolled his shoulders. "You're a Master."

The cyborg drew a pistol and fired. Comet shifted to put BANDIT between them, and the shot caught nothing but air. BANDIT attacked, still raised on hind legs, four arms snaking and darting. Comet caught one and twisted just so. The arm dropped useless. COWBOY uncurled one leg from Shaggy (and Shaggy inhaled, rasping and desperate for air), extended a gun and fired a blaze of shots. One struck Comet in the shoulder, and his arm went numb and spun him off-balance. He retreated, a step again, then another, while turning blow after blow with his one good arm and keeping BANDIT between him and the cyborg. The cyborg saw what he was doing: using her own drones to block line of fire. BANDIT suddenly shot up the wall, driving its piton-claws into cinder blocks. Comet's cover gone, the cyborg and COWBOY unloaded an entire magazine at where he stood.

Had stood. The flare of lights from the guns were blinding, and when the gunfire stopped, Comet wasn't there. He'd gone up the opposite wall. He threw himself at the cyborg, but BANDIT intercepted midair, and the two crashed together. Comet, inside the drone's reach, tore, kicked, and pulled at its soft guts. Red hydraulic fluid sprayed everywhere. They fell eight meters.

The drone had more legs and swept Comet's out from under him so instead of landing gracefully, Comet slammed into concrete. Damaged, the drone landed no better, but its bladed claws dug into Comet's chest armor and lifted and drove him into the wall.

Comet's head whacked against cinder block and his vision went pixilated and lined. *Whack*, again and again. Pain exploded through his head. *Whack*, again, and his hearing went into a high tin-whistle whine.

BANDIT's claws held him in place while COWBOY drew a laser-sighted bead on him that couldn't be missed.

Buzz felt BangBang flee his mind. The cyborg's attacks faltered.

Buzz took the advantage and went straight for what he'd wanted all along. He played man-in-the-middle and tricked COWBOY into thinking that its pilot had requested a video file. Military-quality drones kept a recording of everything they saw for debriefings. It would tell him what happened to JT, Austin, and Dante. He downloaded.

Dimly, outside where the world moved in slow motion, Duke's supersoldier fought BANDIT and Valentine.

She was still distracted away from Buzz. Something about Comet had earned her undivided attention. BANDIT hammered Comet against a wall and held him there. COWBOY cycled a fresh magazine and aimed a killing shot.

Buzz grabbed control of the drone's gun arm, threw its aim to the left, and fired. Pieces of BANDIT went flying, armor useless—it was just that many bullets. Huge divots blew out of the cinder block walls, tracing a path of devastation right toward the cyborg.

—*You care more about your friends than 3djinn,* Valentine sent. —*What a fool.*

—*He ain't my friend.*

She cut their link entirely. The gunfire stopped a moment too soon, and Buzz was alone in his own head, the world gray and peaceful.

The bad guys fled, and Comet slid down the wall to the pavement amid pieces of bot, nothing graceful about it at all.

Valentine and her two drones scattered three different directions. Comet didn't pursue, not even BANDIT, broken and wobbly and missing some legs. He crawled over to where Shaggy lay.

Shaggy looked like hell. He'd looked a bit battered before— bruised eyes like he'd had no sleep for days, cuts and scratches everywhere scabbed over but still red, recent—but now he was positively wrecked. His face was puffy and red from the drone's choke hold. He was flat on his back. He was shaking, and Comet was afraid he was caught in a seizure from whatever Valentine had done to him while they'd been linked.

It wasn't a seizure. Shaggy was trying to laugh. "I got you. I got you, you cocky son of a taint."

Shaggy struggled to stand, but he couldn't even push himself up. Comet offered him a hand. Shaggy batted it away at first, then took it anyway. Standing, he clung to Comet, one arm over Comet's shoulder. The other held his waist like drunken slow dancing. Shaggy's breathing sounded bad the way it did when you've been half strangled.

Comet went a bit hard: Shaggy hanging on him, depending on him the way he was, fucking cute as he was, the way he'd fought her like he had. This was how bad things got worse, this feeling here. This was Duke's fault, the fucker—the dumb-ass orc wiring Duke had given him, and all he could hope was Shaggy didn't notice.

Comet walked him a bit until the guy got his feet under him and Comet didn't feel quite so close to a hard-on.

"You okay? Link me a diagnostic." Because everyone always said they were okay even when they weren't.

Shaggy snapped to his senses and jerked free. He stumbled, fell against the alley wall, and glared at Comet.

"You're welcome," Comet said.

"For what?"

"For saving your damn life."

"You didn't save *my* life. I saved *your* life!"

Comet wasn't going to argue. He'd have been a smear of lumpy red paste on that wall if Shaggy hadn't gone crazy with COWBOY's gun when he had. "You did. Thank you for saving my life."

Shaggy blinked a couple of times. His glare faded soft and apologetic. "Oh. Well. You're welcome. Don't think that means I'm going to blow you or anything."

And Comet's cheeks went hot thinking Shaggy knew about the hard-on. Or maybe he was just talking shit. Comet changed the subject. "Did you get what we needed?"

Shaggy grinned. "I need a place to sit down and analyze it."

CHAPTER FOUR

Long before Buzz had ever met JT, Bruegel had gone deep under. He'd never even said goodbye. It had been the worst fucking breakup in the history of ever.

Bruegel had been Buzz's first: a high-school crush he'd had on an older guy that had soured almost immediately but Buzz had been too stupid to leave.

Buzz had been seventeen, Bruegel nineteen, when he found Bruegel half-naked, skin an unnatural gray shade, sprawled on the bed they shared, plastic tubing spread everywhere, all filled with happy colors that would keep him in a lucid coma and keep him fed. Bruegel would never come back from the digital paradise he'd found.

Buzz hadn't called 911.

That was when he'd become a real hacker, not just a kid messing around. He hacked banks, hospitals, hospices, ambulances, and medical supply companies. He stole more money, equipment, and identities than he'd ever imagined he could. He built Bruegel a multimillion-dollar empire because he had to keep the guy alive and give Bruegel what he'd wanted more than he'd wanted Buzz.

In the end (even today, this very morning at seven o'clock EST on the dot) interns wheeled Bruegel's bed onto the porch of a hospice in the Everglades Islands as if Bruegel could appreciate that there were alligators frolicking beneath him. His bed was more comfortable than the broken-down thing he'd fucked Buzz in, and he was fed all the unpronounceable fluids he needed to stay alive, and there were trust funds that would pay his hospice bills until he was a thousand goddamn years old while his mind wandered the networks and built mathematical castles there.

Months after Bruegel had been safely moved to the hospice, there'd been a knock at Buzz's door. He'd opened it up because he was too fucking tired to care that he hadn't buzzed anyone up. And there she'd stood, holograms of extinct butterflies flickering around her. "I hear you need a new roommate."

He hadn't advertised, so he should have slammed the door on her. He should have been that suspicious. Instead, he'd let her in.

Two weeks later over breakfast, she said, "I know what you did for Bruegel. He was an asshole and didn't deserve it. But he was also a genius, and what you did means a lot to a whole bunch of people you don't know."

Buzz poured almond milk over his puffed rice and didn't tell her what it had meant to him.

Four weeks later, Roan said, "I want to introduce you to some people. They're called 3djinn."

Six years later was now.

Comet's apartment was nothing special. It was a studio on the top floor. It was always too hot and smelled like baked wood. There was a run-down iron-framed bed he'd bought on auction, a bamboo-wood dresser, and a closet filled with so many weapons, explosives, and ammo, his neighbors would have freaked if they'd known. On the dresser were two holo-photos. In one, his parents, anachronistically stoic; in the other, Grandmaster Natalia Jen, faintly smiling in the TRADOC dress blues. Otherwise, the place was practically barren, even the walls. He never stayed here when he was in town. He stayed at Duke's place, where there was a pool and AC that didn't frost over.

Comet glanced out the window, half-expecting to see Valentine waiting on the street looking noir.

Shaggy nosed around the place. He reached for the holo of Grandmaster Jen.

"Leave that alone."

Shaggy did. "Greentown freenet blocks the protocols I use. I'll need access to your network."

"No, you don't." There was no sign of Valentine. Probably she'd gone to lick her wounds and reassess. He pulled the shade.

"Fine. Tell your neighbor, Susan, she should change her password."

"What are you doing?"

"Using her network. Her last name's on the resident's list by the front door. Cross referenced some shit, crawled a few social networking sites, ran her vital stats—birthdays, dog's name, boyfriends, et cetera—through a password generator and boom. It only took about five thousand tries."

"You're a fucking menace. Leave her alone."

"And you're nothing but a wannabe paladin. You don't want me to mess with your neighbors' networks, give me the password to yours."

Comet gave the thief his password and made a note to change it later.

Shaggy said, "Your head's bleeding. You might have a concussion."

"I don't have a concussion."

"She smacked you into that wall pretty hard."

"I was built to be smacked pretty hard."

"Got that right," Shaggy mumbled. He sat on the bed. "Well, you still got blood all over the back of your head." His eyes went half-lidded, and Comet figured he was looking over the data he'd stolen from COWBOY.

Comet touched the back of his head. His hair was all gummed up and sticky.

He went through his closet, pulled out an armored motorcycle jacket he hadn't worn in forever. It might fit the guy. And he dug to the bottom of one drawer and pulled out a pair of jeans from before the accident, when he'd been a couple of sizes thicker through the waist. He tossed the jacket and jeans to Shaggy. It startled him out of his trance.

"You need better protection, riding. Put those on while I clean up." And then he grabbed Shaggy by the wrist, snapped one end of the handcuffs around him and the other end around the bed frame.

"What the fuck!"

"I still don't trust you. And I ain't turning my back on you while you're free."

Comet kept the bathroom door open. He turned the medicine cabinet mirror so he could keep an eye on Shaggy while he cleaned himself up. He shucked his jacket and T-shirt. He ran warm water over a washcloth and dabbed it at the back of his head, and it came away bloody. Head wounds always bled worse than they were. And, yeah, he had a bit of a headache and the washcloth stung and he was achy everywhere like you'd expect from fist-fighting a robot. He didn't check his own medical diagnostic. He was fine. Comet was always fine.

In the mirror, he watched Shaggy glare at the jeans. Shaggy stood and tried to undo his cargo shorts, but the cuffs held his left hand too close to the bed frame and hampered him. He'd have to dress one-handed. He shifted his glare to Comet reflected in the mirror and mouthed, *Asshole.*

Comet gave him an evil grin.

Shaggy turned his back to him like Comet was gonna watch, kicked off his shoes, and dropped his shorts. Comet watched.

Shaggy wore boxers. They were a little threadbare, and the band had lost some of its elasticity, so when the shorts dropped, they tugged the boxers down a bit too, enough to show the top curves of Shaggy's bubble ass and the V of his crack. It was the lily-pinkest ass Comet had ever seen. There was an ass that had never once seen the sun.

Shaggy fought with getting the jeans over his feet one-handed. Fought some more to get them up his legs, hiking up one side and then the other, and finally pulled them over his ass.

Back in 501, Comet had kept a close eye on Shaggy, expecting him to make a break for it while he and Duke reviewed the recording of Jason's place. Maybe he'd kept too close an eye, because bits and pieces of Shaggy stuck in Comet's imagination like the afterburn of headlights on his digital retinas: The puckish slope of Shaggy's nose and the light freckles there. Brown eyes, dilated huge in the orclight. Shaggy's fingernails ragged from chewing. The copper-orange hair on his arms. Freckles on the back of his wrists so sun-thickened they ran together.

Shaggy filled out Comet's old jeans just fine. Really fine.

Water ran in the sink. Water dripped from the forgotten washrag down Comet's back. Comet didn't notice.

Shaggy suddenly turned, and Comet looked away, blinking, eyes gone sticky.

He dabbed at his head a couple of more times and rinsed the rag. The scrapes had stopped bleeding. In a few hours, you wouldn't even be able to find where the wounds had been.

In the mirror: Jeans up and buttoned, Shaggy threw down the jacket he couldn't put on while handcuffed. He dug through the pockets of his cargo shorts and pulled out all kinds of shit: cables, bare chips in blue and green plastic, and a St. Christopher medal sans chain. They said astronauts came back a little messed up, believing things were out there. Net runners were like that too. Prancer carried a hamsa. The ones who spent a lot of time in the net always carried something.

Comet had frisked Shaggy more than once, so none of it was new. It was the usual junk.

Shaggy took one of the chips no bigger than a thumbnail and laid it against the electronic lock on the cuffs. A moment later the cuffs popped.

Comet went still. His body flooded with chems and his senses went sharp. His closet was open, all those weapons right there.

But Shaggy just tossed the cuffs to the side and put on his sneakers. He didn't even glance at the closet. His shoes had laces, which no one saw anymore, and he double-knotted them. Then he took Comet's jacket and filled all the little pockets it had with cables and chips and his medal. Then he scooted back on the bed, sat cross-legged, laid his hands in his lap, and dropped instantly deep into a net fugue, which was as vulnerable as he could possibly make himself, like he trusted Comet not to kill him while he checked out.

And all the while there were the cuffs lying open beside him, like he was saying, *Fuck you and your prisoner shit. Here's what I think of that.*

BangBang had tried to kill him. It was such a crazy thought, it was easier to believe he'd imagined the whole thing. It was easier to believe it was the mouse's fault.

Roan had introduced him to the three that made 3djinn: BangBang (whose handle was technically !!, but that annoyed everyone), Critter (whose avatar was always some kind of small animal, some of them made up, with cute over-sized eyes), and C#Minor (who had no avatar at all). And a few hours afterwards in a shared virtual space, BangBang had watched Buzz with an intensity that bordered on bizarre as Buzz forged an ID. Then it was seven o'clock PST and Buzz closed down.

BangBang had said, "Where are you going?"

"Roan says I gotta get out more, so I got a date."

"Can I ride along?"

"On my date? No."

BangBang wanted full access to Buzz's sensoria, voyeurism dialed to eleven. He'd see what Buzz saw, tasted, touched, heard, everything.

BangBang looked disappointed. "What are you gonna do?"

"Probably we'll jack a simflick together at my place."

"Why would you do that?"

Buzz had laughed. There was a new buddy-adventure sim out that he wanted to try, and it was a lot more fun when a real person played along. You could turn off the simulated sex scenes and do it for real, or do both at the same time. Movie and a blowjob was a perfect date recipe as far as Buzz was concerned.

BangBang stared at him like Buzz was the craziest thing he'd ever seen. "Don't do that. Let me ride along. Your body's in San Francisco? We can go to Fisherman's Wharf."

"Only tourists go to Fisherman's Wharf."

"I want to see the sea lions."

"They smell."

"I want to smell them. Let's go out for ice cream."

"You can sim all that. No. I just met you. You ain't riding me."

The kid went sullen. Buzz said goodbye.

Buzz hadn't understood. The kid (except he wasn't a kid) could sim anything he wanted. At first Buzz had thought BangBang had wanted to ride the (hoped-for) blowjob. That had been creepy, but at least it made sense. But sea lions and ice cream? Who cared about that?

Buzz didn't remember that date anymore.

And it took him a few months, but he'd learned more about BangBang. BangBang was in his late thirties somewhere. He'd gone into deep sleep when he was fourteen. He could have aged his avatar if he'd wanted, but never had. All his experience of the world was sims and cameras and maybe a ride if he found someone who'd let him. A Lord of Shalott accursed in his tower, and Buzz was the closest thing he had to a mirror.

Weeks later, Buzz had closed down his project and BangBang turned to leave, and Buzz had said, "No date tonight. Let's go for ice cream."

Seemed like forever ago, but it had been only two years give or take when Buzz Howdy had been sitting next to JT on that crap piece of a sofa in that crap studio apartment, watching the hologram rotate over the coffee table. The table was scarred by condensation rings like it had a ringworm infection. The holo projector was the most expensive thing in the room, with the exception of Buzz and JT themselves.

Buzz smoked marijuana extract from a vapor pen. It was called Oregon Pixiedelic. It made him feel like rainbows. He passed it to JT. "You sure this is what you want? It's hard to undo this."

JT said, "Yeah," and took the pen from Buzz and inhaled while Buzz stabbed him in the shoulder with the hypodermic and chipped him.

"Congratulations, you're officially Jason Taylor, and ain't no one who can tell you otherwise. You're not a criminal anymore. Worst thing you've ever done is plagiarized your master's thesis."

"Did you have to do that?"

Buzz shook his head. JT had spent his life as a thief and a killer, but he balked at plagiarism. "No one's perfect, *Jason*."

And JT/Jason had grinned that broad grin he had that made having tusks look cute instead of scary, and his eyes went a little glassy from the extract. "I owe ya, Buzz."

An ID as extensive as this one—five government databases, three credit bureaus, and a university hacked and quietly modified—Buzz would have charged anyone else a quarter million. "You don't owe me nothing. It's a favor for a friend."

Buzz took a deep breath, afraid of what he'd see. Then he closed his eyes and reviewed the visual he'd downloaded from COWBOY.

The battle royal went down like this:

JT's drones pile on the Atari named DOC and tear it apart. Turrets mounted on the walls of the compound keep the other two busy.

Through the door of the 3-D printer building comes the strobe-like images of another fight inside: JT cradles a teenage orc girl in his arms and cries. (The girl is his apprentice Dante.) Meanwhile, the elf, Austin Shea, armed with a bow and knives, fights Valentine. Austin is dazzling.

They flee to a car in the lot: a Corvette Dawnstrike FX27. JT lays Dante in the trunk and a single drone climbs in over her, and they tear out of the lot before Austin even has a chance to close the passenger door.

The cyborg stands obscured by the car's dust.

"They're alive," Buzz said aloud. "They got away." He sent a copy of the vid to Comet.

Comet's voice, faint through Buzz's trance: "Where did they go?"

"Don't know yet."

The Corvette Dawnstrike FX27 was a '74 limited-edition car still manufactured by Chevrolet as it had been for the last 122 years. It was print-on-demand, and the licensing fees were in the hundreds of thousands. It wasn't a car either JT or Austin should have. Not legally.

Like any car, it was GPS enabled. The car's location was constantly tracked and registered in the Chevrolet database. If the car was ever stolen, which was highly unlikely given the aggressive (and in some places illegal) antitheft measures that came standard with the car, Chevrolet would share the car's location with local and regional police as well as with the car's owner, who was at liberty to hire whatever paralegal enforcement they felt was necessary to recover their property.

Buzz knew that this car had been stolen by JT's elven friend, Austin, several days ago. It was a quick data check to determine that the only 2074 Corvette Dawnstrike FX27 to ever be stolen was registered to Diego Silva, an LA businessman. Buzz noted the VIN and, using his long-time access to the LAPD/County systems (and the SFPD and the SPD and the PBI and a few others), he determined the car's location as of five minutes ago (the last time the car's location had been updated): lat 35°00'37.8" N, long 105°42'25.1" W.

Route 66, just east of Albuquerque.

Except Buzz couldn't think of a single damn reason why JT or Austin would go east at all. They were both West Coast boys just like he was. Their whole lives were West Coast lives. Their cred was West Coast cred. And, sure, it was possible they might know someone in one of the other North American unions, but someone they would run to when they were being chased by a psycho cyborg and her bots? That didn't seem likely.

So Buzz started poking at the data, which was the thing that Buzz did best.

LAPD/County's data was for shit. None of the ephemerals were there, no packet headers, nothing that told him anything useful. So he went to Chevrolet. He needed the network traffic logs. He didn't have an account, and it would take far too long to social one up, so he sent VIs crawling through the Indigo markets looking for somebody selling and waited.

Comet was still at the sink. The water was running. He was shirtless. He dabbed at the back of his head with a washcloth. A bead of water ran down him: neck to shoulder blade to spine, following a path of least resistance, one seam of muscle on Comet's genetically perfect body to the next, leaving a trail of itself behind it, diminishing itself until the tension between the bead and Comet's skin was greater than its own weight. It stopped a few centimeters above the belt line of Comet's reinforced jeans.

Buzz wanted that drop of motionless water to slide the rest of the way down. It was distracting. He didn't like it just hanging there, waiting for something to give.

One of his VIs chimed. That was faster than he'd expected. It gave him a handful of Chevrolet accounts from disgruntled former employees. IT professionals were always so bitter. He tried all the accounts until he got in. He accessed the network logs, queried the overwhelming list with the Corvette's VIN, and got a subset of the original GPS transmissions.

Among the data recorded in the original GPS location packet was full forwarding route. The first bounce would indicate the cell tower ID number that had been closest to the Corvette at the time. The tower ID numbers he found were nowhere near the coordinates that had been transmitted.

JT had spoofed the car's GPS signal like any good car thief would do. And Buzz had found him anyway, like any good hacker would do.

Buzz gave himself a congratulatory blowjob. It was virtual. He wasn't hung like that, or flexible like that. It was a simstim he'd made when he'd been terribly high and wanted to know if he was any good at blowjobs. (He'd always thought he was, but who ever thought they weren't?) It had been a surprisingly hard sim to make, the editing especially—because the whole thing had been so silly (and he'd been really damn high), it was broken up by recorded bits of his giggling. He played it for a few seconds, both tracks simultaneously, pitching and catching, the way some people played a soundtrack of crowds cheering.

And that was how Buzz knew he was pretty damn good at blowjobs.

He didn't play the part where he came, because often enough it triggered the real thing, and with Comet standing right there, that was the last thing he needed. He opened his eyes just as the taste of his own cock faded.

Comet was running a towel across his perfect back with its perfect muscles and its valleys of least resistance. The towel missed that one bead of water.

Comet reviewed the combat vid Shaggy sent him. And once he was done, he played it again because he could hardly believe what he'd seen.

Comet had fought Valentine and two Ataris, and if it hadn't been for Buzz hacking COWBOY, he'd have died. (He'd give credit where it was due despite his distrust.)

And yet there was Jason, crippled by grief over an unconscious Dante, and an elf with what kind of training Comet didn't know, but it wasn't military and like nothing else Comet had ever seen, and the two of them had held Valentine and her drones at bay long enough to escape in a Corvette.

"The elf is Austin? This friend of Jason's you mentioned? He's good. Who trained him?"

"He's an elf."

As if elves didn't need training, which wasn't true. There'd been plenty of elves at the schoolhouse. Their glamours disrupted lectures and training sessions, and he'd always held the opinion they were only there because they liked the word *ranger*.

"He's good," Comet said, as if what he wasn't really looking at was Jason holding Dante while three utility drones—fucking utility drones!—tore up an Atari urban combat drone.

Duke had always said there'd been something off about Jason—more than meets the eye—and he'd been right. His best friend had been lying to him all along, and this guy here, Buzz Howdy, this fucking hacker, was part of it.

Comet eyed the cuffs on the bed.

"I can't tie my shoes one-handed." Shaggy actually sounded a bit apologetic. "I'd use zip ties next time."

"Damn right I will."

Shaggy slipped on Comet's jacket, and despite it all, fucking God, what a difference a jacket could make. The jacket was a deep-sea blue with yellow trim. Shaggy's hair hung just over the collar. It gave him an edgy look he hadn't had before. Cleaned him up some ways. Dirtied him down, others.

Comet toweled himself off. He did it so Shaggy could see him, all the gentle muscle of him rippling like silk flags. He pulled a clean black compression T-shirt down over his chest. He made sure to do it slowly so Shaggy could watch the fabric stretch.

Shaggy looked away. Comet thought he saw a blush there. "There's another problem." And Shaggy told him about Firelight, the wizard who had hired Valentine to kill them all.

Firelight's full name—his "asshole name" was what Shaggy called it—was Firelight Who Had Stood in the Maw of Abbadon the Red, Was Consumed, and Reborn. Firelight, for short. The way the story went was that Firelight (who was called something else then, but no one knew that name) had freed his spirit from his body and traveled the astral plane in search of wisdom and power like wizards often did. He found himself floating before the Great Wyrm Abbadon the Red and rather than flee (or wake up) like any sane wizard would have done, he dared ask the Wyrm for a small measure of its power. The Wyrm agreed to teach him the meaning of *fire*. It opened its immense jaws and immolated the wizard's spirit, killing him in at least one sense of the word. Firelight awoke from his astral trance with a new name and burning alive, consumed by flames forever.

All of this was just too much for Comet. Seconds ticked by. He finally landed on the only question that mattered: "What does this have to do with Jason?"

"I don't know. I'm just telling you who he is so that you know who we're up against. And I know where Jason and Austin are taking Dante. We have to meet them there."

"If we follow them, we lead Valentine to them. We need to find her while she's still in Greentown and take care of her here. Then Jason will be safe."

"We ain't ever gonna be safe."

"I don't care about you. I care about Jason."

"Fine, you don't care about me. But, look. Valentine is just the tip of an iceberg named Firelight. So let's say we take out Valentine here and Firelight sends his next mini-boss to kill Jason. Except we're not there to help him because we're still here."

Comet searched the hacker's eyes (large and brown and too earnest to be true), looking for the lie there. He didn't find one. "This wizard is that powerful?"

"Did you not hear my story? You don't get away with giving yourself a name like that without being an honest-to-God badass. As long as we're split up and Firelight's hunting all of us, none of us are going to survive, including Jason. But the four of us, together: Jason, Austin, you, and me? We'd have a chance. We'd have more than a chance. The two of us alone . . ." He shook his head, and copper locks fell over his eyes and he had to brush them aside. "We barely beat her in the alley."

And the guy made sense, Comet hated to admit. "Okay. We go after Jason. Where are we going?"

Shaggy hesitated, then said, "Highway 93 north of Vegas. I'll tell you the rest when we get there."

"Just tell me where . . ." and his blood pressure spiked bad enough his combat chems threatened to compensate. He took a deep breath and growled, "This ain't the way to build trust in a relationship."

"Oh yeah, what is? Holding a gun to my head?"

Comet snatched up the cuffs and let them dangle from his finger. "Prisoner."

But he pocketed them instead of snapping them on. He grabbed a med kit and a second pistol and strapped harnesses around his thighs. He stuffed his pockets with four preloaded magazines. Each magazine held twelve bullets. Including the two already slotted in his pistols, that meant seventy-two shots. He took two concussion grenades and tucked them in his jacket. He flipped the lights and locked the door behind him.

In the hall, Shaggy descending the stairs before him, he thought better. He went back. He tossed the cuffs in the closet and shoved a handful of zip ties in his pocket instead.

CHAPTER FIVE

Buzz had a hundred square centimeters for his ass on that bike, a racer with forward seating. That meant Comet was crouched over the battery casing, head tucked behind the tiny windshield, and Buzz was supposed to spoon over the top of him. There were pegs for his feet that were slightly behind his hips, which forced him to lean forward. It was awkward as hell. He wasn't sure where to put his hands. Comet's waist? That didn't feel safe. Nothing about this felt safe. Neither of them were wearing a helmet. Comet said he didn't own one.

He'd ridden on this bike once already from Jason's place to Duke's bar—he'd even been handcuffed at the time—but they'd gone slow and the ride had only been a few minutes, so he hadn't had the chance to build up a good solid panic (or maybe he'd already been so panicked the additional factor of the bike hadn't amounted to much). This was gonna be different.

"You ready?"

"No."

Comet took off, zigzagged a few blocks until they were out of town, and then shot to 200 KPH in five seconds flat. Buzz's hands went from Comet's hips to around Comet, tight. He squeezed and held his breath. Buzz liked roller coasters, so he should have liked this, except roller coasters had magnetic fields and seat belts and shoulder bars, and here there was absolutely nothing to keep him from flying.

"You don't have to hold me like that," Comet shouted. The bike itself made a hooty noise like some old-school UFO. It wasn't loud. The 200 KPH wind was a roar.

Yes, I do, Buzz thought. *Yes, I do. I'll die if I don't.* And Buzz held him even tighter around the waist.

"Unless you want to, I mean," Comet said.

Buzz got the sarcasm just fine. He forced his hands back to Comet's hips.

"Don't lean into the turns. You're throwing my balance. Just look over my shoulder whichever way we're turning."

Buzz was tired of shouting over the wind. "We should link up."

"I ain't letting you anywhere near my fucking head, and you ain't touching my bike."

"I ain't gonna shout the whole way."

"Good, then shut the fuck up."

"You know Valentine can hack this bike, right? The air pressure monitor in your tires is tied to your bike's net by a short-range wireless connection with no security. She can lock our wheels with a thought, and we go flying. I could fix that."

"Short range. She's gotta catch us first."

"You're gonna risk our lives on 'she's gotta catch us first'?"

Comet shook his head like he was arguing with himself, then handshakes, a connection, and that wide-open feeling in Buzz's head like his sinuses had cleared up.

—*I'm watching you,* Comet sent.

—*I bet you are.* Buzz scanned the bike's tiny network and checked config files and logs. These settings felt familiar. He'd seen all these mistakes and security gaps before somewhere. —*This isn't standard. Did you set this up?*

—*Jason did. He made me this bike for my birthday.*

Yeah, that was where Buzz had seen all these mistakes. JT's truck had used settings like this. —*Jason built you this bike?*

—*Jason gave me my life back.*

Jason had shown up at Duke's place on Comet's twenty-seventh birthday riding a custom-built bike based on a Kawasaki design. The bike's carbon-fiber poly molding was red-shifting-to-yellow. Its carbon-steel frame was black. Its four thermos-sized batteries glowed orange.

The orange told their remaining charge. It looked like a fireball. He made voilà hands and said it was Comet's. Comet told Jason he didn't ride anymore. He hadn't ridden in over a year. How Jason had learned Comet had ever ridden at all, he didn't know. He'd never mentioned it. It must have been Duke.

"You don't have to ride it, just sit on it. See if it fits," Jason said, all wicked grin and brazen innuendo.

"I know what you're doing."

"It's hardly a secret."

Comet shook his head. "Jason . . ."

"You'll do HALO drops into hot zones, and you won't touch a bike."

"A HALO drop's never killed me."

"It's only a matter of time."

"You've never woken up and had someone tell you you've been dead."

"Just ride the damn bike!"

"No!"

Comet walked away fuming. Jason walked away fuming. The bike sat there in Duke's driveway for three days.

That first time Comet came back to it, he just stared at it awhile.

The second time, he touched the seat.

The third time, he ran his hands over it and thought to himself how beautiful it was and that Jason had built this for him. And for the rest of the day he'd thought to himself how poor a friend he had been for yelling at him over a birthday present.

And the fourth time, he sat on it, linked up, started it up, and rode it nice and slow down the driveway, feet kicking along, tapping the dirt, saying all the way: *Just to the end, only to the end.* And the driveway turned into the road and the road turned into the dusty highway that ran past Jason's place.

And then he stood straddling the thing in Jason's lot until Jason came out of the printer building wearing grease-covered overalls and cleaning his hands with a rag and some Goop, and Comet took him by the collar and broke the zipper and tore the seams apart he wanted him so bad—it didn't matter that they were just friends now and not dating anymore—and Comet took Jason's sweet ass right there over the bike Jason had built him.

They'd fucked so crazy, the thing went over, and they sprawled over the top of it in a tangle of ankle-binding clothes and plastic and metal jamming into them, and Comet was afraid he'd scratched it all up, but Jason said he'd fix it, don't stop. So Comet didn't and probably that load was the biggest he'd ever shot. He remembered thinking he'd die from that nutting, killed twice by a fucking motorcycle.

A motorcycle's frame was too small for a maglev rig, so they hit the two-lane that ran alongside I-40, and Comet warned Buzz, —*Accelerating.* The pressure of it threatened to shove Buzz off the bike. He held tighter, leaned closer, and the speedometer in his head slid up to 320 KPH and pegged there. Buzz watched the road over Comet's shoulder. It was night. They ran without lights. Comet didn't need them. Buzz couldn't see shit.

And then BangBang came up alongside them on a 1960s-era Harley-Davidson. Buzz knew it was a Harley-Davidson because he'd finally caved and watched the damn movie. In the center of the handlebars sat Critter, a ferret with arms spread wide like he was on the bow of the Titanic (BangBang had made him watch that piece of shit too).

Buzz was still blocking him, but the port range on the bike's firewall that received transmissions was open. Buzz went to close them.

BangBang held up a manila envelope, the universal symbol for data.

Buzz sighed and left the ports alone.

—*I have information you want.*

—*You tried to kill me.*

BangBang didn't answer right away. The Harley roared ridiculously loud. Buzz didn't know how anybody had ever stood the noise of it.

—*It was a medical coma. It wouldn't have killed you.*

—*It would have left me defenseless, and that crazy cyborg would have torn my nervous system out and hot-wired me up.*

—We wouldn't have allowed that.

No, 3djinn wouldn't have, would they? They'd have burned him. They'd have shut him down and then released a virus that would have destroyed Buzz's mind forever. *—You were my friend.*

—I'm still your friend. It was just a little scare. We had to teach you an important lesson, Buzz. Every network's weakest point is physical access. Your body is physical access.

How much of this was BangBang talking and how much of it was the ferret? Buzz tried to believe it was all Critter's fault. He'd never trusted that rodent.

—I've been on my own for years and never had any trouble.

—Because you stayed out of trouble!

—I can take care of myself!

—The way Roan took care of herself?

And that stopped him short, and he went a bit cold because it sounded less like an argument than a threat. And it sounded less like Critter and more like BangBang. And the horrible thought bloomed: Roan had died during a theft gone bad; that was the story he'd heard on the streets. Austin, Roan's brother, told a more paranoid version: he believed the job had been a setup to entrap them. Buzz sent, *—You killed Roan. 3djinn killed Roan because she wouldn't stay in High Castle.*

—Don't be stupid. Roan was the one who showed us how vulnerable 3djinn was. She's the reason we're worried about you. We didn't kill her.

But Buzz wasn't so sure. He didn't know what to think.

BangBang knew Buzz all too damn well. He tempted Buzz with info and waved the manila folder again. *—Your boyfriend's name is Noah Wu.*

—He's not my fucking boyfriend. He's a sociopath who keeps hitting and handcuffing me.

—Boyfriend material, then. I know what you're thinking. You're thinking you and your mercenary, you're going to be some kind of team like Roan and the guys were. But Roan's dead and your friend ain't all that special. I know you want to be a hero, Buzz. But if you want to be the good guy, maybe you should ally yourself with good guys. Here. See for yourself.

The manila folder waved impossibly gently in the simulated 320 KPH winds. Buzz took it and then blocked all the external sim ports, and the Harley and the beautiful dead flat-vid star who drove it abruptly disappeared. Illusion gone, the manila envelope became what it was, a compressed folder labeled *Noah "Comet" Wu.*

Noah "Comet" Wu:

The flat-vid showed the Cambodian dictator Chey Dara addressing the crowd in his 21 March speech six months before he'd been deposed and arrested on humanitarian charges. Behind him stood his personal guard. Name tags read: DONNER, BLITZEN, COMET. Buzz hadn't needed the name tags. He could have recognized Comet anywhere from the way the guy stood: arrogant as fuck, assault rifle across his chest at a perfect forty-five degrees. In the foreground, Chey Dara ranted on about the liberation of humanity. An English translation of the Khmer scrolled helpfully along. It was all the usual filth.

The sudden and violent transformation of some humans into elves and orcs forty years ago had terrified people like nothing else ever had since the Black Death. And there were always people willing to use fear to their advantage. Chey Dara's ranting—the anti-elf, anti-orc, demons-everywhere rhetoric—was stuff you still heard in the American unions. In that vid, Comet's blue eyes didn't show one hint of Jedi. They looked grim as hell.

Noah Wu had been a ranger, 6th Reformed Ranger Battalion, Pacifica, for a few very short weeks. Three weeks after he'd earned his patch—*Rangers lead the way!*—his whole world fell apart. 18 January 2071: court-martial. Charge: conspiracy to murder Grandmaster Natalia Jen.

BangBang hadn't included the judgment on the case.

Buzz knew what BangBang was doing: spinning Comet bad. BangBang wanted him to believe that Comet was a species-ist, murdering fuck, and that Buzz shouldn't trust him.

Had BangBang done the same thing to Comet? Sent Comet a cherry-picked dossier on Buzz—a laundry list of international incidents, leaked documents and video, and criminals who'd entered or fled countries on false IDs he'd created?

No, he wouldn't do that, would he? Too many threads would lead back to 3djinn. BangBang's cowardice pissed Buzz off even more.

Buzz wasn't gonna be manipulated. Buzz knew these games. He'd spent every day of his life since Roan had brought him into the 3djinn fold telling these same kinds of lies, exposing these same kinds of conveniently spun truths, and he was better at it than any of the three. Creating people was what Buzz did. If BangBang was going through all this effort to prove Comet was a dick, then probably that was only half the story.

He released VI crawlers into the web. Somewhere out there was the real Comet, the Comet BangBang didn't want him to know.

CHAPTER SIX

omet piloted them across the Colorado River, though it was barely a river anymore, and through Las Vegas, population 10,462, which seemed oddly precise.

Yeah, people still lived there, if you could believe it, burnt-out lights and quake-broken buildings somehow turned into a symbol of decadent frontierism. Vegas reinventing itself as the same old same-old: still crazy.

He parked at the side of the road for a piss and one final attempt to hail Jason net-wise. It was pointless. Jason was running silent.

Comet gave up and asked Shaggy, "Where to?"

"Keep going north."

"Just tell me where we're going. I'm not going to leave you behind, okay?"

"Say you're sorry."

"Sorry for what?"

"Sorry you held a gun to my head."

"No, I'm not sorry. You were an unknown in a potentially hostile situation. I needed you subdued and under my control."

"Well, that didn't work out so good for you, did it?"

"Just because it didn't work out the way I wanted, doesn't mean it wasn't the right thing to do. A whole lot of things work out like that."

Shaggy glared. "It scared me."

"It was supposed to scare you."

"And you don't feel even a little bit bad about that?"

"No." And Jesus what a fucking lie, but he told it very well the way he always did.

Shaggy squinted at him, ran his hands through his hair.

"No," Comet said again.

Shaggy's hair fell back into his eyes. Shaggy's eyes were huge and chocolate. *No,* shit brown, *those are the words you want to use.* (But that wasn't what stuck.) And it wasn't lost on Comet that even the name he thought of Buzz by—Shaggy—was the label he had given him on his smart gun. He hoped he never slipped and called him that aloud. He didn't think Shaggy would like it very much.

"Of course I feel bad. You think I like threatening people?"

"Yes."

"Sometimes. Sometimes I do. Most times I don't. What I feel doesn't matter. It was the appropriate thing to do at the time, and given the same situation, I'd do it again."

Shaggy sighed. "The Boise Devastation. Take 93 North to the Boise Devastation. Austin's grandfather is a druid. He's there, one of the ones trying to heal the forest after the bomb. JT and Austin are taking Dante there to heal her."

Comet nodded and didn't push for more. He'd won something just now. He didn't know what, exactly, or how, but he'd won and he wasn't going to push it. He threw a leg over the bike and said, "Okay. Highway 93. Boise."

You could barely tell the difference between pavement and the crumbling heat-blasted ground of the Mojave as they drove through. That and the silence between them, Comet and Shaggy could have been on the Moon.

Buzz's VIs returned with their loot. There wasn't a lot.

VI number one had found Comet's family: academics, SF, not ten blocks from Buzz's old place (a lot of California lived within ten blocks of Buzz's old place). The Wu's social media presence was family-and-friends-only and sensibly password protected. He tagged it no-hacking and waited for more.

The desert was blue and nearly shone it was so bright. The horizon was black and gently jagged against midnight blue: hills or mountains or something. For all the tech in him—chips in his head and his humerus and artificial strands running the length of his spine—Buzz had never had his eyes modified. Adding pieces to himself was one thing. Removing pieces was another. So all Buzz had was the moon to see by, and the desert was beautiful.

VI number two found Pacifica Army discharge dates, honorable. That conspiracy charge had gone nowhere, though given the discharge date only weeks after the acquittal, it seemed the accusation had been enough to ruin Comet's career before it had ever started.

They lost their cell tower connection for almost a half hour. There was no government or corporate money or reason to rebuild broken-down towers. Nothing lived here but the spiders, and they had their telepathy. They didn't need wireless.

Along the road ran ancient telephone poles. Or maybe they were telegraph, but hadn't those run along railways? Buzz didn't know ancient tech that well. They weren't power lines, that much he knew. The posts were wooden with wooden crossbars and wires strung along them through ceramic knobs. The wires dipped and peaked, dipped and peaked, kilometer after kilometer.

The bike was going fast. It made its weird UFO-whine, and the wind was constant static. It was like static, wasn't it? That was nice, almost something you could sleep by. It had been so long since he'd slept. And Comet was warm under him.

The bike connected to a working tower, and patiently waiting VI number three dropped its payload.

Medevac onboard vid dated three years ago:

It's a bright sunny day. The 'copter's rotors throw a blurred shadow over desert grass. There are EMTs everywhere. Two are hauling a cryo unit. It looks like a photon torpedo, and it's still spilling vapor. In the background is the perfect black tarmac of a magway and the white of its side road. It's somewhere north of Greentown; he can tell from the desert and the fact the EMTs are all orcs.

Duke Mason is there. The camera positioning is strange: meant to show what's happening outside the 'copter, not inside, so Duke's only on half the screen, and he must be talking to the pilot inside? But he's close enough to the camera/mic Buzz can hear everything he says:

"You're taking him to Lola Benavides at PUCSD." He pronounces it: *puck sid.*

"PUCSD isn't part of our approved provider system. We're taking him where our contract says to take him."

"Dr. Benavides, you fucking shit!"

"Sir, step away from the—"

Duke's eyes shoot sparks in a lightning-storm way Buzz has never seen before. Duke roars and those gold-inlaid tusks flare with sunlight and the white-blue from his own eyes. They flash the camera blind for a moment, and then Duke reaches past the camera with an arm big as a tree and plucks that hapless pilot right out of his seat and chucks him a good ten meters.

EMTs scramble, shouting. The two with the cryo unit load it onto the 'copter as if nothing is amiss. Someone tasers Duke. Duke doesn't notice. He hits the guy so hard his helmet flies off. They pile on him with stun batons, useless on a frenzied orc. Duke fights them all. He curses everyone. He weeps. The deep-wisdom valleys of his face catch tears and glitter in the sunlight. He shouts, "Comet! Comet!" the whole time.

For just a moment, Buzz thought Duke was calling Comet for help.

Buzz closed the file before the vid ended, not wanting to watch any more.

Before he lost this tower, he gave his VIs a new quest: Dr. Lola Benavides, People's University of California, San Diego.

Their network connection cut in and out.

Road signs Buzz couldn't read, just saw the rectangle shapes of, flashed by.

The wires on the poles running alongside the highway went a bit crazy. They split and arced down and back up and crossed everywhere like some old lady's shawl, poorly knitted with too little yarn.

—You see that? Buzz sent.

—Old webbing, don't worry.

Silver broken strands hung from black wires.

Buzz tried not to worry.

Something on the network: faint, just a hint of traffic, maybe nothing, maybe not. Buzz accessed a rear camera, saw nothing. The network dropped. Then it came back, and the net was still as glass. He stayed linked to the camera and waited.

There it was again, just a flicker.

—There's something behind us.

—There's nothing behind us.

—Something on our same net.

—Settlers or something.

There were always people crazy enough to try to live somewhere people didn't belong. *—Maybe.*

—We're pegged at 320. Nothing goes that fast except us.

—Plenty of things go as fast as we do. Any Ferrari or Bugatti, a whole bunch of muscle cars, there's even a sixty-year-old Cadillac almost as fast but it ran on gasoline. The Namir Plainstalker drone can sprint at 350 for three minutes. Any helicopter, peregrine falcons—

—Falcons.

—When they dive-bomb, yes. And five roller coasters: Abu Dhabi, Shanghai—

—You're kidding me.

—Cincinnati, Paris—

—Fine, you keep watching for roller coasters.

—And Brussels. I will.

—You do that.

—I will.

Dr. Maria de los Dolores Benavides Owens, in residence at PUCSD Hospital, was an expert in the manipulation of pluripotent stem cells. Comet had entered her care less than twenty minutes after the motorcycle accident that had killed him.

She and a team of scientists had revived him and had not only regrown everything that needed regrowing, but had reprogrammed his genetic code using a targeted retrovirus technique that was common for some cosmetics purposes—the kind of purposes popular with porn stars and midlife-crisis divorcees—except Comet's genetic reprogramming had been far more extensive than that.

The medical record had a huge number of images. Buzz didn't have the stomach to watch them.

Comet had lost control of his motorcycle, and the bike had slid some fifty meters before coming to a stop. He'd slid seventy. There were places where the fabric of his jacket had gotten so hot from the friction it had melted to him. His face had been unrecognizable. How had his brain survived? Was it possible to rebuild it? Rebuild it from what? He had to have huge gaps in his memories.

Buzz, used to technologies that were practically magic, had never seen something like this. Comet, rebuilt, was some kind of Frankenstein's monster.

Except Victor Frankenstein had never loved his creation, and Buzz had no doubt that Duke loved Comet deeply.

A different story, then: Pinocchio.

Did Comet even know the lengths to which Duke had gone to bring him back to life, the favors he'd called in, and the money he'd spent? That would explain Comet's devotion.

But that didn't feel right. Comet didn't know, did he? Comet didn't seem like the kind of person whose devotion could be bought. He was devoted to the man who mentored him because that man deserved devotion. Probably he'd been devoted to Grandmaster Jen the same way.

Buzz tried to imagine loyalty like that. BangBang and 3djinn?

Jesus fuck no.

Roan, and JT, and Austin?

Yes, them.

How was it that everyone in the world seemed to be loved by someone except him?

CHAPTER SEVEN

Travel Advisory: Gamma Spiders

When the network presence came back, Buzz sniffed it. He got a bit of information, enough to guess he was detecting a vehicle's subnet, and then the presence vanished. Someone had detected his snooping around and turtled up, disconnecting themselves from the network entirely. That wasn't the kind of thing normal people did.

Buzz released a squad of VIs to comb the network—spies and informants—reinforced his own firewalls, and made sure the tires were patched.

He felt the bike slow. He snapped out of his trance and sent, —*I don't think this is a good time to slow down.* Then he saw what lay ahead. "Oh shit."

They stopped. Everything went weirdly quiet without the sound of the electric engine or spinning chain or wheels on pavement. The moon had risen full, and the webs in front of them glowed beautiful and silver. No longer the random single strands that had decorated the utility poles and wires for the last several kilometers, the webbing here draped in huge sheets across the highway, bound together by threads thick as powerlines, a spun mass, a great tent, a pavilion for some fantastic emperor, suspended from wires and posts and running farther than Buzz could see in the night. The husks of dried sage and lavender hung in it, blown there by the wind. A tunnel ran through the mass. It was ragged, as if something huge like a semi or something fast like a Corvette had plowed straight through and kept going.

"Can we go around it?"

"It's a light bike, but I don't know about off-roading with someone on the back. That ground out there looks loose."

"Can you see the spiders? Your eyes, I mean."

"Spiders are endothermic, and the webbing is just as radioactive as the spiders. Everything glows."

"Radioactive? How radioactive? I'm just a normal human, remember."

"Is that what you are? You'll be fine. This webbing looks old. I think we'll be fine."

Buzz looked behind them and saw nothing but darkness. But if it was Valentine behind them, she wouldn't need headlights any more than Comet did. The network was quiet. His VIs waited. *A bit like spiders*, he thought, and that made him shiver. "All right, then, let's go."

Comet took them through. The road was straight, but the webbing hung in tatters everywhere and heaped on the pavement like old blankets. He wove the bike back and forth between all of it. The webs were old, just like he'd thought, but if any of them were still sticky, they could mess up the bike.

He scanned the silver walls and ceiling for signs of movement. Moonlight filtered through the threads. Sounds were strangely muffled. The webs smelled of old forests and dust. From time to time, the webbing cleared, and they'd be under moonlight for a split second and then back within the long silver tube. Behind them, their wake made the whole place tremble. The stirred-up wind pulled brittle webbing free. Light as air, the sheets spun, dervish ghosts, and were long out of sight before they ever touched ground.

Comet didn't like it. Gamma spiders were attracted to movement.

Through the heat sensors of his rear camera, he saw the hot, square shape of a car. That was almost a relief—not spiders, at least—but the car was running without headlights. —*Car at our six*, he sent to Shaggy.

And maybe Shaggy tried something then because the car sped up, closing the gap between them meter by meter—the red, orange, and yellow-white glowing block of its engine getting larger and brighter in his camera eye.

—*It's her!* Shaggy sent. —*Go faster!*

Comet tried, but there was too much debris in the road, too much hanging from the ceiling above. He slalomed through it, best he could. A sheet of webbing brushed his arm so lightly he didn't even feel it, but it clung to him. Behind, the car didn't even try to dodge the piles of tattered silk. It plowed right through it all.

He passed his pistol's slaving to Shaggy, and he felt the guy pawing at his thigh holster trying to pull it free. The car came closer. It was immense, blocky, as un-aerodynamic as a car could be and nearly half engine to compensate. It was silver by moonlight. Its hood ornament, the Spirit of Ecstasy, flickered hologram-blue above a tangled RR logo. The ornament was animated, so her winglike gown billowed behind her. Valentine was trying to run them down in a goddamn Rolls-Royce.

Shaggy shifted his weight erratically, trying to turn to get off a shot, still too afraid of falling off the bike.

The car grew closer and closer, ten meters, eight, six, five. Headlights came on, exploding blindingly bright.

—*Fire, goddamn it!* Because if that thing so much as tapped their rear wheel, they were going down.

They punched through webbing, Comet not caring any more than to get ahead of the Rolls.

The pistol thundered. A single divot and a spiderweb of cracks appeared in the windshield. Shaggy cursed blue. The Qayin was a high-powered pistol made for a hulk of a soldier, or someone genetically restructured. Shaggy was neither. He'd had to shoot one-handed, and it was a miracle he hadn't dropped the gun or broken his wrist.

Comet hit webbing. It stuck to the front of the bike and over his face. He tried to tear it away, only to tangle it everywhere.

The Rolls was too close, a meter behind. Shaggy shot and whined through the network about his wrist. The windshield cracked more, but didn't break.

No more space, no more time, the Rolls was upon them. —*Hold on,* Comet sent, swung left, and braked. The Rolls howled past them and tried to sideswipe them but missed and plowed into the thick webbing of the walls.

The damage rippled through the delicate structure, and Comet could feel the questioning pressure of the spiders' telepathy on his skull.

Windshield draped with webbing, still Valentine didn't stop. She didn't need to see to pilot the car. She had cameras and sonar.

The trunk of the Rolls opened. Robotic eyes glowed from the crack: BANDIT and COWBOY. Gun barrels slid out.

Comet sent, —*The tires. You said they were a vulnerability. Can you hack her tires?*

—*Short range.*

—*How short?*

—*Half a meter.*

Half a meter? That little shit. He'd made it sound like he could do it a kilometer away. —*Get ready. Give me the gun.* He ignored all Shaggy's sputtering protests.

The rear wheel was too close to the bots, so Comet went for the front. BANDIT and COWBOY opened fire as Comet swung right.

Comet hit the gas and zipped up the passenger side of the Rolls. The passenger window came down the way Comet expected.

The spiders' telepathic pressure in his skull went white hot, and alien images flooded his mind: crazy web-spun geometries like it was spells the spiders wove, palaces of silk, spires adorned with arachnid banners.

Comet and Valentine unloaded their pistols at one another, unable to aim, both of them locked in the pain of the spiders' psychic assault, all spray, bullets wild. The Rolls jerked right and slammed into them, pinning Comet's leg between the car and bike. The car forced him to the edge of the road even as the bike slid up the length of the car to the front wheel. Webbing battered him as they skimmed the walls of the tunnel. They trailed veils. Glowing shapes moved within the walls.

—*Now, Shaggy now!*

And then just like that, the Rolls disappeared behind them with a rubber-burning screech as Shaggy locked its brakes and blew its airbags for good measure.

Shadows, dim, many-legged, and glowing faintly with radiation, swarmed the Rolls. The psychic pain subsided, and then all that was behind them. The spider-spun tunnel ended and opened to sky. Comet accelerated, bike whining terribly like it shouldn't.

"You did it! You did it!"

The afterwards rush hit Comet hard, even harder than in the alley. Adrenaline energy with no place to go blended with the strange sexual wiring Duke had given him. Comet went hard and against all his better sense, every instinct told him to pull the bike over and celebrate. And maybe that was what they needed to sort the two of them out. Comet shook his head, fighting the fuzz of sex and endorphins and adrenaline. This wasn't the time or the place for a hard-on. There was no room for it in his jeans. There was no room pressed against the body of the bike.

Shaggy took care of it. —*I think I've been shot.*

CHAPTER EIGHT

Travel Advisory: Cannibal Country

On the right side of the highway was an ancient single-story motel. The sign said *MOTEL*, as if you couldn't tell what the building was. The sign was dead. The lot was empty. Most of the windows were broken. Some of the room doors stood open.

On the left was a fueling station, a Phillips 66 so old it didn't even have hydrogen. It had the old gasoline pumps, though the tanks buried under them had probably not held gasoline in thirty years. It had one building: a service garage. Its walls were reinforced with extra plywood and corrugated metal sheeting. Surrounding the building was a graveyard of cars abandoned during the Second Zombie Apocalypse. They had prices painted on their windshields. Comet couldn't imagine who there was to buy them. Beyond the fueling station was nothing but scrubland.

Comet turned the bike into the Phillips's lot, and a sharp chemical stink hit him. He stopped short.

"What's wrong?"

"Land mines."

"How do you know?"

"I can smell the explosives."

"In the road?"

"No. Out there," he said with a nod to the land around them. "And a whole lot more in that garage."

Shaggy leaned out and scanned the darkness. "What's out there?"

Comet saw nothing either. "Dunno."

"We should keep going."

"I need to take a look at your arm. And there's something wrong with the bike." The bike's self-diagnostic was flashing yellow and red lights in Comet's head.

They both looked at the garage. The whole place smelled like rust. A breeze sighed through the burnt-out signage and broken-down cars: a lovely, eerie, hollow whistle.

They both looked behind them, fearing headlights.

Shaggy said, "Do you think she survived?"

It seemed hard to imagine. Between the spiders' telepathy and her broken-down Rolls, it didn't seem like anyone could have survived. "Hell yes, she survived."

But what else could they do? He kicked the stand down and they slid off the bike. "Take off the jacket. Let me see your arm."

Comet took the first aid kit from the bike. Shaggy winced when he tried to take the jacket off by himself, so Comet helped him.

"Can we turn on the headlight?" Shaggy asked because they were working by the glow of Comet's eyes alone.

"No."

Shaggy took off his flannel overshirt too, and there was a nasty bruise that showed black by Comet's blue eyes. No puncture though.

Comet sighed, relieved. The jacket had done what the jacket was meant to do.

Shaggy saw the damage and smiled.

"You know you've been shot, right?"

"I know." He showed his arm to Comet like Comet hadn't seen it, and his grin was pain-hazed but it was broad and dimpled and V-shaped and proud as fuck. As if in Shaggy's squirrelly head, getting shot had been a rite of passage.

"Ain't never been shot before, have you?"

"No."

Comet snorted a laugh and smiled also. He picked up the jacket and stuck his finger through the scar the bullet had made, dug into the pulverized insert, and there it was, deformed a bit and caught in the fibers. He dug the bullet out and gave it to Shaggy. Shaggy put it in the same pocket of the jacket where he kept his St. Christopher.

Comet told him to wait here, and he walked slowly toward the service station's garage. He could smell the chemicals of the explosives even buried. Software translated the odor into a visual overlay.

He'd taken barely ten steps before a voice called out, "I wouldn't do that if I were you."

Comet turned. Beyond Shaggy and the bike, in the middle of the motel's lot, stood someone with a high-powered flashlight. The glare made it hard to see, and Shaggy was shielding his eyes with his good arm. Comet's eyes filtered the light until he saw the man clearly. He was a worn-down-looking man, older, bearded. The flashlight was duct-taped to a shotgun.

"Land mines," the man said. "You two ain't cannibals, are you?" He glanced at the bike. "No, y'ain't. You got bullet holes in your bike." As if bullet holes were proof of a socially acceptable diet.

More than bullet holes scarred the left side of Comet's bike. The molding covering the engine was shattered and hanging by one loose bolt. Webbing gummed up everything. How the bike was still running, Comet didn't know.

"Spiders," Comet said to the man.

"Spiders with guns. Damned things just keep getting smarter. And here everyone thought it would be the cockroaches what took over."

He lowered his gun and came toward them.

Comet said, "You seed those mines?"

"Yep."

"What for?"

"Ghouls in the hills. Like cannibals, but crazy and desperate. Don't care how long you been dead. They're running out of graveyards. Send scouts down from time to time. I keep the lights off and they forget I'm here. When they remember, the mines remind them to keep away. You're safe long as you stick to the highway."

"Why do you stay?" Buzz asked.

"Where else would I go?"

"Almost anywhere."

"We need to repair the bike," Comet said.

"Aye-ah. Maybe I can help with that. Whaddya got for trade?"

They negotiated a few Hooah! bars and ten antibiotic tablets from Comet's med kit in exchange for the man repairing the bike.

Comet asked, "You got running water?" and the man nodded to the motel. Comet said to Shaggy, "You clean that arm up. Put some paste on it."

Shaggy sent to Comet, —*You trust him?*

—*I don't know yet.*

Shaggy got some all-purpose med-paste from the kit and started for the motel. Comet stopped him. He filled a hypo with life monitors. The tiny nano-bugs would swim around in the guy and detect all kinds of things. "Should have done this before."

Shaggy pulled away from him, scowling, but then relented. Comet injected the bugs.

Buzz rubbed where he'd gotten the shot. He stopped at the highway's edge and said, "This safe?"

"You walk straight that way and it's safe," the man said, and Comet confirmed, no mines there.

Buzz crossed the parking lot, eyes on the ground like he could see the mines. The life monitors reported his heart rate had skyrocketed, and he calmed again only when he disappeared inside a random motel room.

Comet watched the station attendant work on the bike. He watched the road to the south for Valentine. He watched the hills for ghoul scouts. And he watched Shaggy's vitals. Five minutes later, Shaggy's breathing went soft and even, and his heart rate slowed and steadied. Comet shook his head. Comet was out here on high alert. Shaggy was taking a nap.

Comet sneezed from the mildew. The light in the bathroom was on. Low wattage and failing, it barely lit anything. On one of the twin beds, Shaggy slept sprawled flat on his back. He looked like he hadn't lasted a moment. He lay at a curve, one leg on the bed, the other dangling off the side, one hand resting over his chest, the other curled above his head. His breath whistled through his freckled nose.

Comet lifted Shaggy's leg by the cuff of his jeans (Comet's jeans) and set it on the bed. He thought maybe he'd take the guy's sneakers off at least, but he didn't.

So now look at him sleeping there.

The guy was a con man, a hacker, a low-life. Comet didn't want to think that Jason had friends like this. Jason couldn't have friends like this. People like this weren't friends. They were slime. And the cuter the package, the slimier inside.

Except Shaggy had saved them twice now, hadn't he? In that alley, he'd let Valentine jack into him, a calculated risk to get the data they'd needed, and that took some nerve. It was the kind of thing Prancer would do on a battlefield network, the kind of thing Comet would do. A low-life crook with nerve like that? A low-life crook proud of taking a bullet?

Goddamn, look at him sleeping there.

That's my jacket on him. Those are my jeans. And someone wearing his clothes, it was almost like touching them. It was enough to give him the shivers. Comet's jacket would smell like Shaggy when he took it back. It would smell acidic like his sweat, sharp like the mint in his hair, and sweet like fading pot, and Comet would be able to slip on those smells, wrap himself in them like he was wrapping Shaggy around him. And Comet's jeans would smell like Shaggy too, the dirt and sex of him.

Comet nudged the bed with his foot. "Hey, time to go." He didn't try sending. Sending to a sleeping person gave weird dreams.

The bed shook a bit from the nudge, but Shaggy didn't wake up. So Comet knelt beside the bed and tapped him on the shoulder.

Shaggy's eyes fluttered half-open, and his hand caught Comet's wrist. Hypersensitive, life monitors magnifying, Comet could feel the even beat of Shaggy's heart through his fingertips.

"How long was I asleep?"

"Fifteen minutes."

Shaggy let go of him slowly. The AC wasn't working and Shaggy's hair had gone curly and deep copper with sweat. A lock of it stuck to his forehead. He furrowed his brow to dislodge it, and before Comet could really think what he was doing, he brushed it away for him.

Shaggy blinked his sleepy eyes at him.

"You had hair . . ."

"Oh."

His were beautiful eyes: milk chocolate, with thick and bronzed lashes. Lips exactly that right shade of pink, and Comet leaned closer, so close he could feel the hot stream of Shaggy's breath on his lips. *Damn it. Damn it. Damn it.* He closed his eyes and brushed his lips on Shaggy's. The very tip of his tongue slipped past his own lips and pushed into Shaggy. Shaggy let him, and he tasted just a bit sweet, like the memory of bubblegum.

He's a criminal, he reminded himself. *A villain.*

Can a villain taste like bubblegum?

Duke will be pissed.

Damn it.

The Reindeer will have a fucking field day with me.

He tastes like bubblegum.

Damn it.

Comet pulled away. He sat on the edge of the bed, ready for Shaggy to come to his senses and push him away (because Comet wasn't going to come to his senses). He felt a bit dizzy.

Shaggy beetle-browed. "Is this a good idea? I mean, usually when a guy kisses me, next thing that happens is someone shoots at me."

"Really?"

"Well, it didn't used to be that way, but recently, yeah."

Comet stuck his finger into the scarred material where the bullet had hit Shaggy. "You already got shot, so you're owed one, right?"

Shaggy smiled. "Yeah, that's right. But I'll keep the jacket on, just in case."

And Comet liked that idea. Fucking this guy while he wore nothing but Comet's jacket—yeah, he liked that idea a lot. He dove at Shaggy, attacking those lips, needing to know how all of him tasted: lips, eyelids, the tip of his nose, the curve of his ears. He ground his hips against Shaggy's leg. Their fingers entwined and held so tight he was worried he was hurting him. Comet sucked at the softness beneath Shaggy's chin (where not three hours before Comet had shoved a pistol, and if he opened his eyes and looked, he'd see the semicircle bruise that he'd made).

And he didn't care what Duke was gonna say, or how all the other Reindeer were gonna laugh at him. Donner would tease him for being seduced by his prisoner; Blitzen would tease him for taking advantage of his prisoner, and he didn't care either way. He didn't care about anything but this guy who smelled like bubblegum and pot and had brown eyes gone eclipsed with needing Comet, and lips all brighter red now that they were flushed with blood and wet with Comet's spit and his own. And Comet slid an arm beneath him and lifted him up so they were sitting, legs in a tangle, so he could feel the swell of Shaggy's cock against his own.

He whispered Shaggy's name—"Buzz"—between sucking and kissing and tracing him out with his tongue, practicing the word so when he came in the guy he wouldn't say "Shaggy," wouldn't have to confess it was the name he'd told his gun, though it meant so much more now. Except Buzz wasn't his real name, was it? No one could be named Buzz Howdy. "That ain't your real name."

Buzz laughed, puffs of breath against Comet's neck between kisses. "And Comet ain't yours."

"What is it, then? What name do I say when I'm coming?"

Shaggy's kisses slowed. Then he untangled himself from Comet. "Everyone calls me Buzz."

Damn it. Goddamn it. Comet should never have asked. He'd pushed too far too fast and fucked this all up and should never have asked.

Buzz said, "You wouldn't like me if you knew anything about me. You already don't like me."

"I— That's not—"

"The Blue Unicorn—that hologram you saw at Jason's place, the AI fragment I told you about—I stole it from a triad a few days ago. They told me it had a glamour, which isn't supposed to be possible, except it did, and they wanted me to reverse engineer it so they could use it in pornography. And I said yes. And then I saw it, and I realized I knew it. It was modeled on the memories of an old friend of mine, Austin's sister, Roan. We think that somewhere out there is an AI created by her and the Blue Unicorn was a piece of it."

Buzz sat cross-legged on the bed, same as he'd done back at Comet's Greentown apartment. He fidgeted with the hem of Comet's jeans that he wore. "So I stole it. And Jason and Austin helped me. And when we finally got away, we set her free. And that was supposed to be the end of it, and I was supposed to go . . . well, away . . . but she came back to Jason's place, and I followed her, but by the time I got there, Dante had already been hurt, and Jason and Austin were already gone, and then you showed up . . ." He scowled. "And you held a gun to my head."

Triads? The sex industry (and not the good kind, Comet guessed)? And hadn't he heard stories about a gang war three days ago on Telegraph Hill of all places? Shaggy in the center of it all.

And maybe it was just too hard to imagine, or maybe he didn't want to, or maybe it was because he'd already known that Shaggy was into some bad shit and Comet had gone ahead and kissed him anyway, or maybe it was because Comet was hardly no saint neither, but it all didn't make a bit of difference.

And the voice in his head (that always sounded like Duke) said: *No, it's because you're a romantic, Comet. Because you believe in love at first sight and soul mates and love conquers all. And no matter how much the world shows you otherwise, you want to believe in good guys and happy endings. Because you're a dipshit.*

And I believe my gut, Duke, and that's why Reindeer Squad's alive. And my gut says this guy ain't a villain and maybe he ain't a hero either, but he's something. I don't know what. Something I want to find out.

"Well?" Shaggy said, like he'd been waiting for Comet to walk out and leave him there.

"You're still pretty fuckable." Jesus, was that the best he could do? Shaggy scowled.

"And . . . well . . ." Comet did his shoulder roll and gave Shaggy a faux shit-eating grin, shy and ornery all at once, all braggadocio the way he used to be. "I'm pretty fuckable." He wagged his thumbs at himself.

"Is that what you are?" Shaggy wasn't smiling, but Comet thought he saw the barest flicker of one, the faintest hint of a dimple quickly fought down.

"Maybe not just that."

"Yeah? What else? Besides an asshole."

All the showmanship fell to the wayside, because Comet really didn't know. "What else do you want me to be?"

You hold two magnets apart from each other and close your eyes and feel their attraction. You feel the strange humming slide of it between your fingers, and it seems to grow and grow and grow until your fingers can't hold plus and minus apart.

"I don't know, yet," Shaggy said.

You have to let go, and those bars of metal snap tight in midair.

Snap: jackets a slick rasp of ballistic fabric, hands to clothes, clinging, tangled in hair. Mouths against one another furious; lost seconds like they'd been lost years. They were going to hurt one another. They were going to press themselves into each other like they were one body, some beautiful experiment in teleportation gone perfectly awry. God, there'd be bruises when they were done, deep purple bruises, God, subcutaneous blue, God, whatever it took as long as they were one.

He heard soft pops like tires on road debris, and light flooded the hotel room's sole window, throwing slatted lines across them and against the wall. In the back of Comet's mind he'd been aware of the service attendant working on the bike, but now the attendant was gone. And Comet realized he'd made a serious mistake letting his attention wander from where it should have been. They both turned, and the glow went blinding as the source approached fast.

"Aw, shit," Shaggy said. "See, I told you."

Comet tackled Shaggy into the narrow gap between bed and wall. He expected a hail of bullets. What he got was a Buick at 60 KPH.

The front of the room crumpled like wet cardboard under a ton of plastic and steel. Their feeble bulb in the bathroom blew. The car plowed right into one twin bed, then the other. The mattresses buckled, and the old, dry pine frames shattered. And all of that wreckage slammed into Comet and Shaggy hard enough to drive them five centimeters into the paneled wall and pin them both there in the darkness.

The car's engine clicked. Broken wood creaked. Ceiling tiles rattled free from their framing and fell on the car and the ruin of the beds. The carpet they were trapped against smelled rancid.

—Buzz, are you okay? Buzz?

—Yeah, yeah, I'm fine. Shaggy struggled a bit. *—I can't move.*

Comet shushed him and listened. He didn't hear anything that sounded human or robotic. He squirmed under the pressure of the mattress and threw his elbow back into the wall behind him. The drywall and wood popped and cracked. A couple of more blows and the thin wall gave, and he pushed his way into the bathroom. He hauled Shaggy through the hole and held a finger to his lips. He gave him a pistol.

Shaggy held it in both hands pointed at the floor, which was probably just something he'd seen done in some cop sim and he looked ridiculous doing it: this cute little guy playing badass soldier. But Shaggy's eyes were dilated huge, his heart rate and blood pressure were up. He was sweating, breathing shallow, and life monitors gave Comet a list of all the natural endorphins and adrenaline flooding his bloodstream. This wasn't no game, and Shaggy was scared.

—I can't see, Shaggy sent.

Comet dialed up the glow of his eyes, and the bathroom's dingy ceramic reflected the pale blue. Shaggy nodded, calmer now.

—Stay behind me.

Comet looked around the bathroom door out onto the wreckage of the room. The mattresses and frames and blankets and pillows were squashed against the wall. The battleship of a car was barely scratched. Even the windshield hadn't cracked. The driver's seat was empty. It had been piloted drone-like.

The car suddenly lurched backward and hung up on something. It rocked, then lurched again and pulled itself free and out into the parking lot. The front wall of the room was completely gone.

Through it he could see the Rolls parked in the middle of the highway. Its headlights were on. Valentine paced in front of the lights, a black silhouette, raincoat and broad hat casting immense shadows. COWBOY and BANDIT paced alongside her. The air was filled with dust from the building collapse, giving the headlights and shadows a thick liquidity like it was the light from some hellmouth with its resident demon rising through.

Shaggy sent, *—She's between us and the bike.*

—I know.

Outside, Valentine shouted, "I know the two of you are still alive."

That hole in the wall was a deathtrap. Comet looked around for another escape, but there were no other windows or doors. Then he noticed the drop ceiling, and through the damage he could see that the hotel walls didn't go all the way to the roof.

He stood on the toilet and sink and pushed a tile up. He vaulted up to the narrow ridge of the wall separating rooms and pulled Buzz up behind him. Ductwork, wiring casements, and rafters filled the space and ran the length of the hotel over all the rooms. The ties and latticework holding it together looked fragile as hell. They'd have to crawl carefully or they'd fall through. Comet moved the ceiling tile back into place.

Valentine's shouts were dull but still audible. "You know what I should be doing right now? I should be tearing your motorcycle to pieces and stranding you here so I can cruise in luxury all the way to Boise. Firelight offered me twelve million to kill you, Buzz—you, JT, and Austin, plus the orc girl, unfortunately for her. Yet here I am talking."

They slowly crawled their way along the rafters. They tried to avoid the ducts, but the space was shallow, less than a meter, and the rafters were triangle braced and hard to maneuver around, so they had to use the ducts to keep from falling. Comet moved silent as dust. Buzz didn't. The ductwork creaked, and even the soft contact of his knees on it sent dull thuds echoing.

The tiles were rotting and broken. They fit the suspension latticework poorly and light from the Roll's headlights wavered through cracks.

"I'm hoping to make a deal. Comet, you give me Buzz, and I'll forget I ever met that wizard. I'll back right out of that contract. I'll walk away and pretend I never heard of any of you. JT, Austin, Dante, the Blue Unicorn, any of you. Just give me Buzz Howdy."

Shaggy's crawl slowed, just a stutter in his movement. And he tried to hide it, but Comet caught Shaggy's sidelong glance at him. And then Shaggy kept on, but that sidelong look had stung.

—*I'd never do that,* Comet sent.

—*I know.* Another meter of crawling. —*I'm sorry. I've had two friends try to kill me recently, and I knew them a whole lot better than I know you. Or I thought I did.*

—I'd never do that.

—I know. He sounded more confident that time.

The thin filtered light from below wavered. The Buick was moving again. *—I wish she'd turn off those goddamn headlights. The station guy said lights attract the ghouls.*

—They must have heard the noise already.

They passed over another room.

Outside, tires squealed. The Buick rammed their ruined room again, and the whole building shuddered. Comet held one of the power conduits for balance and Shaggy's jacket with his other hand.

Silence afterwards, no way to see what was happening below them or outside. The claustrophobic blue glow of Comet's eyes reflected off billowing dust.

Comet looked at the conduit in his hand. *—This motel's smart?*

—Yeah. Out-of-date by about thirty years, but smart.

—Can you hack it from here?

—Wireless is off. You give me a wire, sure. But why?

—I want you to turn the lights on. All of them. Bright as they'll go.

—Is that a good idea?

—No.

—As long as we're clear on that.

Comet broke the conduit sheath with his hands and began sorting wires. Shaggy fished through his pocket and produced a cable that would work to patch him in. Outside, Valentine continued to tempt Comet. She told stories about 3djinn and Shaggy and the work he had done in the past and who he'd done it for. Comet ignored her as best as he could, but he could see the tension in Shaggy's shoulders.

Shaggy patched himself in, and the motel's lights blazed.

Valentine stopped talking midsentence.

—If nothing else, that was worth it.

They started their clumsy crawl again. They passed over three more rooms.

The Buick rammed the motel a third time. Everything shook. Structural groaning turned into a roar. Rafters shifted and braces bent. Buzz slipped and his hand went right through a ceiling tile, and the rest of him nearly followed. Comet caught him by the jacket, hauled him back up to the rafters.

The building cracked and trembled. They scrambled, careless, to the end, as the building collapsed behind them.

They dropped down into the motel's registration. —*Stick to the walls. Watch your shadow,* Comet warned. Shaggy parted the blinds with two fingers and looked out the window into the lot. Comet peeked over his shoulder, keeping farther back so the dim glow of his eyes wouldn't be seen from the outside.

The motel was L-shaped. The short wing held the registration desk and back offices; the long wing, the rooms, most now collapsed. Between the two wings was the lot. It was lit like downtown. Alongside the fueling station sat Comet's bike, a hundred meters away, gleaming yellow and red behind a field of battered old cars. It might as well have been in another state. There was no sign of the old man.

The Buick pulled free of the motel. Debris came with it. A wrecking ball couldn't have done better.

Valentine scanned the building. Her wide-brimmed hat threw her face in deep shadow. Her cybernetic eye glowed dully through the darkness. COWBOY and BANDIT rotated their heads slowly. Targeting lasers played over surfaces.

And everybody waited for the other to make some move.

The seconds passed into minutes.

Comet started to think it wasn't going to work. Then the first explosion rattled the blinds.

From behind the motel: a flash of light and a plume of dirt and smoke. COWBOY and BANDIT shot that way, COWBOY leapt up the debris of the building and over. BANDIT circled around, passing so close to the window they watched from that they both crouched, afraid it would see them. Valentine, smart enough to sense a diversion, moved closer to Comet's bike. It sat there like bait.

The rattling and popping of gunfire came from behind the motel.

—*How long do we wait?*

Shaggy was getting edgy. Comet put his hand on Shaggy's shoulder to calm him. —*When I go, you follow, and keep low, okay?*

—*Yeah, yeah, okay.*

More shots, different direction now. Another explosion, the flash of it over the motel. Another and another.

—*Jesus, how many of them* . . . and then Shaggy trailed off.

—*Oh shit,* Comet sent.

They came around the far side of the motel. They came around the near side. They came over the top. Some drove jeeps and ATVs and more clung to the sides. Most simply ran or climbed.

They were human and alive, not zombies, but their eyes were pale and wide, and their nails were long. They screamed and howled battle cries and spun hooked nets and shook machetes. They weren't careful where they drove, and some were run over. Those behind took the time to stop, but not to help their injured. Their machetes hacked, and they left mounds of broken bones and chopped meat and ran on swinging limbs over their heads like trophies.

Shaggy stepped back, pale and wide-eyed.

COWBOY and BANDIT ran with the ghouls, firing into them. They flung nets in return, and those did more to hamper the drones than guns or knives did. The drones' legs tangled and they fell. The drones cut themselves free as ghouls dog-piled them and beat them with clubs.

Comet sent, —*Now!*

—*I'm not going out there!* and Comet had to drag him away from the window and out the door.

Across the highway, more lights blazed as all the old, beaten-up cars in the station lot came to life. They inched forward, all of them at once. Their tires suddenly spun and squealed and they lurched toward the ghouls. Valentine had taken control of them all, each one a half-ton weapon under her command.

The highway and lot became a demolition derby like nothing Comet had ever seen. Ghouls ran everywhere, cars spun and battered into each other, some drifted too far and triggered mines and the vehicles bounced a meter into the air on a column of smoke, guts blown sky-high.

Comet smiled at the bedlam stink of it. This was perfect. This was better than he'd hoped. And though he'd never admit it—not even to Blitzen in his most drunken moment—this here felt like home.

He counted deep breaths with Shaggy to help calm him because the hacker was on the verge of panic, then they ran out into the maelstrom. So much chaos, so much smoke and dust kicked up, they didn't bother to hide. They held hands as they ran because if they were separated, neither would ever find the other again.

Something struck the motel sign. It tumbled and crashed in a spray of sparks, and ghouls cheered and lights flickered everywhere.

Behind a car, overturned and smoking, Comet told Shaggy to stay there and hide.

—Where are you going? But he did as he was told, huddling in tight to the dirt-caked chassis.

Comet disappeared into the smoke and dust.

—There's a stockpile of mines in that garage, and I want them. There's a bridge ten K north of here. We're going to cross it, and then we're going to blow it up. It'll take her hours to find another way across the river.

Buzz flinched with every single explosion, no matter how far away. He'd never been in a war zone before. He didn't even like to sim them. And sure, he'd been chased by killer helicopters at a druid's lodge, but that had still been nothing compared to this. He was shaking, so pissing-himself scared that it wasn't hard at all to just stay and hide. He held the pistol in both hands and aimed it at every looming shadow or strobing headlight that pierced the dust. He fought the urge to ask Comet to keep talking just so Buzz would know he was okay and coming back.

He didn't belong here. BangBang had been right—Buzz should be somewhere safe while Comet did the heroics. He was nothing more than a hostage crisis waiting to happen.

Another explosion, and he pressed tighter against the axle of the BMW. It was a BMW; not one of the ghouls' dune buggies or jeeps, but one of Valentine's cars turned up on its side. And there he was, right beside it.

Maybe he could be worth something after all.

—Comet, I'm gonna try something.

—No. Stay where you are. I'm on my way back.

—It'll just take a minute.

—I said stay where you are!

He dug in his pocket and found a small chip: a wireless adaptor. What were the chances Valentine would drop one of her wrecked cars from her network? In the heat of the battle, she wouldn't think of that, would she? If he could access it, he could access her.

The air vibrated with gunfire, shouting, detonations, and screams, the sources all lost in the smoke and night but for flashes. He tried to climb the car to the window, couldn't with his hands full, so tucked his pistol down the back of his jeans.

One leg over the car's side and he was high off the ground and exposed.

Something lashed out of nowhere and wrapped his arm: a handmade net covered in fishhooks. It tangled around the sleeve of Buzz's jacket (Comet's jacket). It jerked tight and yanked him from the car. He landed hard, wind knocked clean out of him, stars everywhere.

A ghoul, horror-show fresh, dragged him by the net. Two more rushed him with nail-studded clubs. He fished for his gun, but it had been knocked free. The locator told him where it had fallen, and he tried to scramble for it, but the net held him. He tried to untangle himself, but the hooks just dug into his hands and deeper and tighter into the jacket sleeve.

They raised their clubs two-handed over him, and he screamed and kicked.

Comet appeared amid darkness and dusk, Jedi eyes blazing, and shot all three—*bambambam*. He cut the netting from Buzz's arm in one slick move. He helped him up and held him closer than he needed. *—Are you okay?*

—Yes.

He wanted Comet to yell, *I told you to stay put!* or something like that, but Comet didn't. He only looked worried and relieved, and that was so much worse than being yelled at.

Comet scooped up Buzz's pistol, and they ran through the crashing and explosions and choking dust. Slung over Comet's shoulder was a burlap bag, two cylinders the size of small coffee cans inside. Buzz pocketed the chip, no point in it now if they were leaving the dead car.

The smoke parted, and there stood the bike and the Rolls and Valentine. Her coat flared as she turned on them, but Comet was the faster shot. She dove behind her Rolls. A trail of fist-sized bullet holes tracked behind her as Comet fired.

—*You're driving!* Comet told him.

—*I don't know how!* Buzz was a San Francisco boy. He'd never learned how to drive anything.

—*I'll guide you.*

Buzz straddled the bike and brought it to life, and he prayed to no one in particular to let him do this one thing right. Comet tapped his senses the way porn stars did, the way BangBang did when he was riding: sharing just a hint of proprioception and equilibrium and vision. It felt like a sigh—and he let Comet guide him the way someone might guide the hands of an inexpert pool player, intimacy impossible to ignore. He felt like they overlapped.

This was the reason people learned to play pool.

—*Go, Buzz, go!* Comet unloaded the rest of his rounds at Valentine and the Rolls in a steady stream meant to keep her down. Even with Comet's help, Buzz almost spilled them over first thing, but he kept it upright and it became easier the faster they went. Comet fired two last shots at Valentine and they tore back onto Highway 93.

CHAPTER NINE

Gray in the east, break of dawn.

Behind them, Valentine had extracted her drones and her newly slaved cars from the melee. It had taken her minutes and each minute that passed had given them more of a lead. Valentine's vehicles or the ghouls or both had triggered mines and explosions boomed. Comet had cheered silently with each one and hoped that one or the next got her, but the liquid chrome surface of the Rolls was unmistakable behind them. It didn't matter. She'd never catch them now. It was only a few minutes to the bridge, and if it was half as much of a wreck as the satellite images showed, the two mines Comet had stolen and were now slung over his back, placed correctly, would be enough to drop the whole thing into the canyon.

Shaggy kept the bike upright. Their speed made it easy, though Shaggy was nervous, as nervous as Comet had been that first time he'd piloted it. He touched Shaggy gently through their shared space, and felt—or imagined he felt—Shaggy smile, the way you could with people you guided.

And then, of course, the engine stalled entirely. They coasted for a half second and lost speed. Then the engine kicked back in with a lurch that nearly made them spill. Diagnostic alarms sounded.

Shaggy's shoulders tensed up.

Comet sent, —*We'll make it. Only seven K to go.* It was only one stutter. Valentine and her fleet were a few hundred meters behind.

A fleet of twenty cars swarmed around her Rolls. She formed them into a pincer, with her fastest cars at the tips, Buick in the center, and the Rolls-Royce two cars behind it. The crescent spread wider than the highway itself and spewed hot contrails of Idaho dust.

Formations facilitated control over large numbers of drones by allowing the controlling mind to reduce sets of variables to one, the same way astrophysicists were able to reduce the Earth's gravitational source to a single point rather than distributed across the entire mass. The cars' movements were uncanny. None waited for another to get out of the way. They all moved at once, a single living thing.

The gray horizon went to orange like they were speeding along Mars, yellow sun through dust. Dust writhed across black asphalt, the illusion of priceless watered steel, perfect.

The bike stuttered and stuttered again. Lost speed again and again: 250 fell to 230; 230 to 210. Comet cursed the bike. He cursed Jason for building something that broke when it was shot at, like Jason should have fucking known when he'd made the thing that a cyborg with a whole fleet of cars would chase them from one apocalypse into another.

—*We ain't gonna make it, are we?* Buzz sent.

—*We're going to make it,* Comet said, without believing it himself.

Fifty meters behind them, BANDIT and COWBOY sprang from the Rolls's trunk and bounded from hood to hood, one to each tip of the crescent formation.

—*Drop the mines?*

—*She'll see them, and they'll miss. But if I'm close enough, maybe . . .*

Aloud, he mumbled, "'I'm gonna be an airborne ranger. Live a life of guts and danger. Airborne ranger, guts and danger. I'm gonna be an SF medic. Get me some funky anesthetic.'"

—*Are you singing?*

He wouldn't have called it singing. It was some bit of memory from better times. Something to center him. —*My mantra.*

—*That's not a mantra. That's "Airborne Ranger."*

—*That's my mantra.*

—*What are you doing?*

—*I'm going to go back there and slow her down.*

Silence.

—*All you have to do is just keep going down the road. Nothing fancy.*

Shaggy sent, —*In my pocket's a wireless adaptor. Let me feel your fingers.* And Comet opened himself wide to the hacker. There was nothing left that they weren't sharing. Comet felt through the pockets.

—Not that. Not that. That! There! That's what I was trying to do at the hotel. Comet, I'm sorry. I shouldn't have—

—You can hack her the way you did before?

—No. Not her. The cars. They're old. Old security. If you get the chance.

He didn't think he would. He took the adaptor anyway.

The bike stuttered again; 210 to 175 and Valentine's swarm closed fast and eerily quiet like a sandstorm. The cars were so damn near now, Comet could feel the wash of heat from the road pushed forward by them.

—Steady. Steady. You got it. You're doing great, Comet sent. He chanted, mocking, over their network, *—I wanna be a cyber jockey. Stealing porn from my Kawasaki. Airborne Ranger, guts and danger. Cyber jockey, Kawasaki.*

And he leapt from the bike.

You didn't become Grandmaster Natalia Jen's favored student by having a crazy streak. You did it through discipline, focus, and drive. Comet's crazy came later, after he'd died and come back. Or maybe it had always been there, and this new body Duke gave him just meant he didn't have to hide it anymore.

It wasn't magic, what Comet did. It wasn't even what Jen had taught him. When he'd gotten his eyes, he'd learned that what everyone said was true: technology eroded your qi, and he'd had to learn everything over again. So he couldn't fly, not like he used to, but he could jump really fucking high and fake the rest.

Directly behind them was the Buick Valentine had used to ram the motel, still in one piece: his target.

The height of his jump gave Valentine too much warning. Valentine braked the whole fleet of cars, just a tap that threw Comet's timing.

He landed one foot on a bumper held by one bolt. That final bolt gave, and the whole piece vanished underneath, twisted and flattened and shattered just like Comet should have been, but that one foot had been enough. So instead of his dramatic three-point landing guns blazing, instead of getting crushed by twenty cars, he was flung across the Buick's hood. He let momentum roll him into a somersault, and twisted so that he slammed back-first and sideways into the windshield. It buckled under him. Shatterproof, it didn't break.

At their crescent points, COWBOY and BANDIT's mantis heads whipped around, abandoning Shaggy for the more immediate threat, laser-beam eyes seeking.

Comet leapt up, pulled one mine from the bag because one mine popped near that Rolls-Royce and the fight was over and they were free.

Except COWBOY and BANDIT saw it and opened fire. He had no time to throw.

Comet bounded the three meters to the Hyundai Daisho next to him. Valentine flexed the formation. She juked it left and right so Comet landed on a moving target, had to work to keep balanced, no chance for a good throw. He carried the mine like a football in the crook of one arm as he jumped to another. The drones chased him with bullets and skipped across cars themselves, one car to the next, trunk to hood, hood to hatchback, glass and plastic bursting and tearing. The wind whipped a spray of debris behind them. Comet landed on the tail end of an old Volvo; BANDIT landed with him and COWBOY on a Kamugen sedan alongside.

He tried to leap again, but BANDIT snagged his pant leg and hauled him back down. He hit the hood hard with a *whump*, and the sweat-slick mine went flying, and no scrambling after, no wild flailing let him catch it. It disappeared amid the cars. He sent the command and popped it anyway, nowhere near the Rolls, but any damage was better than none. A car bucked and shimmied off the highway. "*Fuck!*" he shouted. He'd wasted one of his mines.

The swarm closed in. If they managed to get in front of him and encircle him, all they had to do was slow and Shaggy would be forced to stop, and this would become a fight they wouldn't win.

Buzz tried not to watch. He tried not to let each explosion or fusillade behind him draw his attention from the road. He focused on Comet's life monitors, everything elevated the way they should be given what he was doing. Buzz had troubles of his own.

Valentine hammered the bike's firewall. Buzz shrugged it off. Valentine proxied attacks like an amateur. They were all fake. Valentine was no amateur. They were taunts and distractions.

The road decayed rapidly as they neared the gorge. Chunks of turned-up asphalt rose like old-time glacial shores. He wove past, getting the hang of it now.

Ahead: the bridge. God, that chasm was deep. There'd been nothing like this fifty years ago. One apocalypse after another had wracked this land, and the Snake was the new Colorado.

The bridge was a truss bridge built sometime after the apocalypse that had cleft the river chasm into a land-borne Mariana Trench. And then had come The Bomb. The bridge was two lanes and in the worst repair a bridge could be and still be called a bridge.

Two K away. Thirty-eight seconds.

Balanced on the hoods of shifting, swerving cars, the drones on either side of Comet attacked hand-to-hand as if Valentine couldn't help but show off. Comet ducked some blows, side-stepped others, blocked the rest, and they came so fast and hard, the impact-proof plating in his jacket began to break down. He struck back, precision strikes at the drone's joints and hydraulics, where they were the weakest.

His fists slammed into BANDIT and his torn-up knuckles left red-smeared dents. BANDIT stumbled back even with four legs, and Comet kept up his attacks, pounding and kicking. Its claws dug into the car as it slid off the hood.

The cars veered crazily beneath him as Valentine tried to save her drone. It didn't work. BANDIT fell and was crushed beneath everything.

No time to celebrate: COWBOY attacked while he was off-balance, arms unfolding and striking so hard they'd have broken bone on anyone else, bouncing Comet car to car.

Around Buzz, cars closed in, the formation tightening into a column anticipating the two-lane bridge.

Twenty seconds.

Comet slid across slick hoods uncontrolled. He grabbed for purchase on anything he could. He caught a handful of glass from the Buick's shattered windshield, and the windshield gave. He was back where he'd started. He threw himself into the car as gunfire sprayed where he'd been.

Her cars were everywhere around Buzz, ahead and to the side, and he finally realized what Comet must have known all along and would never admit: their plan wasn't going to work. She'd cross the bridge with them, and they weren't going to escape.

Fifteen seconds.

Comet rolled into the Buick, down to the floorboard. Bullets tore through the car's roof and side windows, and everything above him vanished into the wind, torn away. One bullet struck the armored plating in his jacket, and it felt like an elbow to the back.

He pulled the wireless adaptor Shaggy had given him free from his pocket and looked for a place to slot it—nowhere, nowhere, nowhere, fuck's sake, was this car that goddamn old it didn't have a jack?—and then there! And *click*.

Above, COWBOY blocked out the sky.

Network access was better than weed, better than any god damned thing on this earth.

—Get out of there, Buzz told him because she was his now. She hadn't bothered to update the ancient cars' outdated security, and now Buzz was gonna fuck her up.

Five seconds.

Everything lurched as Shaggy took control. The car behind the Buick rear-ended it with a *bam,* and the Buick veered another direction.

COWBOY hauled Comet from the Buick, held and punched and kicked him, leaving him bloody. Comet wrenched himself free of the drone, but too late and not enough. COWBOY filled him with bullets, all Valentine's fury in a few hundred grams delivered at kinetic energies meant to kill cars. Bullets slammed into his chest. The carbon plastic of his vest pulverized. Capillaries burst and ribs cracked and the wind was blown out of him as his muscles spasmed tight and unmoving.

Around him, cars rear-ended one another and shot off different directions. Bumpers tangled. Plastic flew. Shaggy had fucked with every damn car in the fleet, turning wheels, braking, and speeding up others. He didn't have land mines, but he had cars, and Buzz threw every goddamn one of them at the bridge. Some cars shot off the canyon edges like two-ton missiles and struck rusted supports, which gave. Some funneled onto the bridge harrying the Rolls. They smashed through barricades and broke through guardrails and fell and drew ancient pylons down. Shaggy's vengeance: havoc.

Comet barely registered it at all. His world, already dim with dust and pain, strobed with thick shadows cast by the twisted ruined bracings passing above them. He couldn't breathe. He felt weightless. He was falling. He barely felt the impact, that pain nothing compared to the rest. He clawed out because instinct demanded him to claw. His vision cleared. He hung from the finger-raked roof of a car, and there loomed a mantis-shaped robot over him, child-painted COWBOY. It had the detached hood of a car in its grip and it swung it down on Comet, *bam*!

Comet's fingers, if not broken, numb, couldn't hold.

Bam, one more time.

—Comet! Jump, goddamn it, jump, came Shaggy. But there was too much dust and too much blood in his eyes, and even if Comet could jump, he'd lost all sense of direction and didn't know where. All around him cars were upended and wrecked and thrown into the abyss.

And now COWBOY aimed his gun, and what could Comet do?

—Don't stop, he sent, *—Don't stop,* and let go.

COWBOY's endless bullets tore the asphalt decking. Comet was swept away.

Buzz saw Comet fall. Through the cameras of a dozen dead cars, he saw Comet roll and keep rolling and rolling and still rolling like all the laws of physics were broken now, and Comet's body would die forever because Buzz had been too careless.

Comet's life signs went erratic, stayed erratic for one long second, and then dropped to levels Buzz didn't trust could be real.

—Your knight has fallen, Valentine sent because their networks were joined now.

My knight. My knight. She shouldn't have said that. The only man he'd ever met who hadn't betrayed him even when he should have. *My paladin.*

And finally, in the middle of the broken bridge, surrounded by smoking cars and rubble, girders falling, swinging wildly, all the bridge's support blown out from under, Comet's terrible roll came to an unnatural stop, and Buzz understood the anguish that had fed Duke's rage when he'd seen Comet like this before.

Buzz passed off the bridge onto dirt, no highway this side of it. He slammed to a stop and spun a one-eighty with a rooster tail of dust.

Or that was the plan.

In real life, no great pilot, he swung out in a tepid left arc. His wheels slipped across sand and rock, and he nearly laid the whole damn bike on top of himself.

But Comet lay hurt in the middle of that bridge, and Buzz wasn't going to leave him, not ever. There was no thought of anything else in his mind—not JT or Austin or Dante or the Blue Unicorn—there was nothing that mattered but Comet, downed.

Valentine's beautiful car—a car like an angel would drive—followed him off the bridge, followed him in his long arc across the open ground, and not a fleck of dirt stuck to its mercury surface; even the bullet holes Comet had given it seemed to accent its perfection.

The bridge was clogged with cars and rubble Buzz could never hope to thread, so Buzz dropped the bike, laid it flat on the ground. Gravel dug up his pant leg when he fell, shredded him, and he didn't notice. Behind him, the Rolls crept up on him, inexorable, nudging cars out of the way. Buzz couldn't stop her, so didn't even try. He ran back through burning cars and broken steel supports and leapt spans of buckled concrete, and the bridge quivered and shook.

Comet was a dust-covered ball, barely recognizable, hair matted, dirt-caked blood everywhere. Buzz tried to haul him standing. Comet kicked and fought, trying to help, making a mess of it all, and they both fell. The bridge wavered.

Around them whirled dust clouds high as Mount fucking Everest, and its thin gaps made everything all the more hellish. The morning sun, high and hot, blazed hazily like a demon hating down on some alien surface. The world smelled of carnage: choking dust, hot asphalt, and oil. Buzz begged him, "Comet. Please stand up. Comet, please."

Comet's hair was dull orange, breath shallow, heartbeat low, and temperature high. He pulled weakly at the shoulder-slung burlap bag until it came free.

The Rolls-Royce stopped amid the wreck of her fleet, not two car-lengths away. Its door opened. Valentine's heel struck the span. COWBOY scrabbled up behind her, metal legs clacking. In her hand she held a small cooler, brain-sized, the kind of cooler black-market docs used to store organs. It steamed nitrogen cold. Buzz could feel it from here. The heels of her boots clicked across the crumbling concrete as she came nearer.

Comet clumsily freed the mine from the bag, and Buzz thought, *Better that than what she'll do to me.*

But Comet threw the mine. It rolled to one side. Neither Valentine nor COWBOY bothered to stop it. It was nowhere near them.

"You missed," she said.

The mine kept rolling and rolling until it bumped up against a steel pylon.

Comet held Buzz's hand. *—We're going to be an airborne ranger.* The mine exploded.

Maybe Shaggy's massive car wreck hadn't destroyed the bridge, but he'd damaged it so badly all it needed was that one final push.

Steel buckled. Concrete disintegrated into gravel. Spans of asphalt crumbled. The bridge fell into the Snake River, one huge, long, grinding, apocalyptic fucking Götterdämmerung crash. The whole thing plunged down like the Bifröst between worlds, and the universe rent in two.

Valentine didn't cry out or shriek when she fell into the abyss, COWBOY falling too. She fired her pistol at them blind with hate until she ran out of bullets.

Comet flew. He flew like he hadn't done since he'd gotten his eyes. He flew like he'd never done, ever before.

Noah Wu remembered the strike that had done it. They'd sat in the breezeway that wrapped the training yard, and the regiment banners lining the halls were still.

And he struck the bell.

Except it wasn't a strike at all. It was barely a breath. It was only a breath. It was *qi*, nothing but steam over rice. And hearing that sound—that tin ring of a bell untouched but fantastically rung like the heroes of old could do—Grandmaster Natalia Jen had closed her eyes in joy. So few of her students had done it before him.

It was one of Comet's finest memories of her: eyes closed in joy.

If she could have seen him now.

Comet took Shaggy by the hand, barely touching, fingertips to fingertips, Comet's breath already entwined with his, they needed nothing more, and he flew. His toes barely touched the rubble that fell past him. His one free hand only gestured at steel girders falling past, and, as if he'd gripped them, he flung himself upward. He climbed, and he climbed, touching nothing but the man he loved. He climbed faster than gravity could pull the bridge down. He climbed faster than despair could drag them down. He climbed faster than hope could lift them. And if Comet had climbed any faster, he and Shaggy would have become paired stars in the sky.

CHAPTER TEN

Travel Advisory: The Boise Devastation

The Second Zombie Apocalypse had hit Boise hard. Pacifica, Christian Texas, and New Atlantic had jointly bombed the fuck out of the place. CTexas had used a low-yield nuke. (Try explaining that to the internationals. But everyone, even the Russians, knew CTexas was batshit.) News outlets had claimed "We got 'em!" but stories to the contrary resurrected every few years, and the crazy Geiger counts spun the rumor mill: Morse code from the dead. Every few years, someone published a translation of the ticks. Necromantic cults flourished in waves, complete with the inevitable Kool-Aid suicide pacts.s

Great, more walking dead.

Then came the druids. Plants versus zombies. And they did pretty good. Radiation levels plummeted, so everyone turned a blind eye to what those druids sacrificed to convince the forest to forgive the bomb.

Welcome to Boise.

Flat on their backs, they lay there a moment and waited for the worst. The worst didn't come. She didn't rise over the ridge riding the back of COWBOY (which was a dream Comet would have from time to time). Valentine was gone and dead.

Comet wanted to fuck.

He felt like absolute hell. He couldn't remember the last time he'd hurt as bad as this. And he couldn't remember the last time he'd needed to fuck as badly as this. He wanted Shaggy now.

They were still holding hands. Just now, that was the best he could do. Shaggy's hand was warm and surprisingly strong, and he wanted to never let go.

They lay there together at the broken edge. They both stared at the sky because they were too tired and too beaten up to turn their heads, not even to one another. The touch of their hands had to suffice, and the blue they saw in the sky was the kind of blue meant to write rainbows upon, not a single mote of dust to obscure it. They started to giggle. Comet had never giggled in his life. That was how messed up he was just now, that he would giggle.

"You saved my life," Shaggy said.

"Yeah, that was cool. I was really cool. I wanna fuck you." He suspected he'd pushed himself just a bit too far and wasn't thinking quite right.

"I think that would kill you."

"Yeah, I can barely move. I can't fuck anything. You saved both of us."

"No, this was all my fault," Shaggy said, a whole lot less giggly. "I need a joint."

Buzz pulled a spliff from his jacket (Comet's jacket) one-handed and tucked it in his mouth. He dug in the pockets some more and flicked a lighter.

A druid extinguished his flame with the tap of a fingerlike branch and rumbled, "Only you can prevent forest fires."

Modern-day druidism had less to do with historical druidism and more to do with spiritualized environmentalism. The world was filled with spirits. Two thousand years ago everyone had known that. A hundred years ago, science had winnowed that population to hardly anyone. Today no one knew what to think, except the druids.

The druid was nine feet tall and crowned in antlers—not worn, but grown. It was robed in bearskin and armored in wyvernhide, and its staff was a birch tree. It brought up old memories that Buzz couldn't have, magically formed: green men, forest kings, and white stags. Behind it stood wicker-made creatures. They were tangles of twigs and fur with stripped bark as string to hold them together. There were bears and deer and horses and raccoons styled like they'd stepped off the walls of Lascaux or Chauvet. There were stick people, faceless. Woodwoses.

Comet struggled to his feet, fists balling, looking ready to fight. Even without the medical feed, Buzz could see just that bit of effort took everything out of him, and Comet nearly fell.

—*Comet, stop, you need to rest.*

—*As soon as everything stops trying to kill us, I'll be happy to lie down for a year.*

The druid didn't try to kill them. It looked over the wreckage, what remained of the bridge, and sighed. "You're friends of Austin Shea."

"Is it that obvious?" Buzz said.

"Darkness chases you everywhere."

Buzz rolled his eyes. "Are you Grandfather Henry?" The druid wasn't an elf, but neither was it an orc or a human. It looked like nothing Buzz had ever seen before.

"I am Urushiol. I lead this circle. Henry has gone."

"Gone? I thought he was the leader here."

"Not anymore. I will take you to Austin. You will finish your business here. Then you will leave."

It gestured with its birch-tree staff and two trees separated themselves from the woods behind it and, cracking and groaning, crawled their way on writhing roots toward them. Their branches split and curled and formed into claws, and it was clear they were going to pick them up and carry them.

"We can walk," Buzz said.

"You will not." Urushiol said. "We have suffered enough trespassers on our land, and we will suffer no more."

Fifteen minutes later, the trees lowered them to the ground. After the swaying of the tree, Buzz felt a bit off-balance. There was a break in the landscape, a sudden jagged cliff like the same earthquake that had jacked up the Snake River had also broken the land here. A tall, narrow cleft struck through it—a deep cave.

"JT and Austin are here?"

The druid pointed to the cleft, and then it and the band of creatures and trees returned into the forest. The sounds of their passing—the rattling of branches and whisper of leaves—melded with the rest, and they were gone.

Buzz and Comet ascended the last few dozen meters to the cleft and went in. Comet pulled his pistol and dialed his eyes brighter, and Buzz was gonna say, *It's just JT and Austin,* but this hadn't been at all what he was expecting, so a pistol might be a good idea after all. *—Can I have one?*

And Comet passed one to him.

Roots and vines hung from the roof of the entrance tunnel. It smelled like living things. Like when Buzz imagined farms, he imagined smells like this, like a really nice vegetable garden written large.

Comet led. Buzz let him.

The passage bent gradually right.

Something dropped from the ceiling, big and metallic, reflecting blue in Comet's Jedi eye-shine. *COWBOY!* Buzz panicked. The cave flooded with white light, and Buzz, vision spotted, tried to fire into the glare, but the pistol wouldn't do anything. Comet had shut it down.

"Buzz, it's okay, it's Jason!" at the same time JT said, "Buzz? Comet? What the fuck are you doing here?"

The cave was huge. The immense roots of the trees above shot through the whole thing like stalactites, some so long and powerful that they pierced the room ceiling to floor. Buzz couldn't see the walls. The only reason he could see anything at all was the magical glow at the cave's center. Oak leaves and motes of gold and green light swirled around two sleepers: Austin and Dante.

JT crouched just outside the whirlwind of magical leaves. He was forest green and wore jeans and a firetruck-red T-shirt. His tusks were stubby, and he worried one with his tongue. His eyes were bruised and sleepless, irises huge, no sclera visible, and flecked with orange, which meant he was worked up, nerves on high alert.

Beside him sat the utility drone that had dropped from the ceiling of the cave entrance and spooked Buzz. It was four-legged and unarmed. Unarmed maybe, but JT had brought down one of Valentine's Ataris with a pack of them. The way it crouched there beside JT made it look like a vicious and protective dog.

Dante was someone Buzz had never met, only heard of. She was an orc girl. She wore fashionably torn-up jeans held together by safety pins and a pink T-shirt with a dead pony on it. Her hair was a long Mohawk, dyed purple, and one of her tusks was broken off short.

Austin was an elf on the heroic side of elves, beautiful as fuck, and the kind of vain prick you'd expect to cause a world war, some cross between Fëanor and Helen of Troy. He was dressed in the same thing he'd worn yesterday when Buzz had seen him last, which made him look like he was slumming, and not like the slob he actually was. God, Buzz hated glamour.

Austin and Dante lay side by side, his left hand in her right. Austin's right hand lay over his chest, curled around a short ivory wand that sparkled like someone had dusted it with glitter.

Not a wand. A unicorn horn. *The* unicorn horn.

The horn didn't look like what Buzz had imagined it would. He'd imagined something long and spiraled, tapering to a point, silvery-ivory white. He'd gotten the color right, but that was all. It was only twenty centimeters long. It wasn't thick at all, barely a solid twig of a thing. And he realized the reason it didn't look like he'd expected was because it had been filed down, shaved everywhere like a cheese block on a grater, and what Austin was holding was only the core of the horn, all that was left after Grandfather Henry had used it to heal his people so long ago.

The three stared at each other a long time. JT's mouth twisted like he was confused by them being there; then he frowned like he was pissed off by them being there; then he grunted like it finally all made sense, and he bit his lower lip like now he was ashamed. "I was supposed to pick you up at the airport."

Comet said, "It's okay, I caught a cab. You're exhausted."

"I'd have been there, but something came up."

"Yeah, we know. She chased us all across Nevada."

"She's here?" JT's eyes went wide, and his drone scrambled back to the cave entrance.

"She's dead," Comet said.

JT stopped his drone. "Valentine's dead?"

"Comet dropped a bridge on her."

"Valentine's dead." JT shook his head as if he couldn't quite believe it. His drone returned to his side. He reassessed the two of them. His gaze lingered on Comet's cuts and bruises, torn clothes, and dirt-matted hair. "I should have known you'd come after me."

"Yeah, you should have," Comet said. The accusation in his tone was gentle but unmistakable: JT hadn't trusted Comet with his secrets and Comet was hurt.

Buzz couldn't blame him, and maybe now was the time to get it all out in the open. "I've told him everything, mostly."

And then Buzz told JT the story, getting him up to speed. He left out a few parts (so, no, maybe not *everything* out in the open, not yet). He left out the kisses and hand holding and pelvis grinding and not a word of what they'd have done after the bridge except they'd both been too exhausted to do it. But he told everything else.

He looked at Comet nervously, wondering what Comet was going to say about his version of the story because he knew JT and Comet'd had something between them once, and he wasn't quite sure what it had been or what it was now. And he wasn't sure if he and Comet had something between them or not. And he wasn't sure he was ready to know.

And just now, this very moment, he desperately wanted Comet to say what he couldn't: *Buzz left out the part where we kissed.* But Comet didn't say that, and Buzz felt mildly and unreasonably betrayed by Comet's support of his own omission.

JT nodded and sighed, relieved by the story, and looked over at the two people sleeping deep within their spell, "We're safe, then."

"I don't think so, JT. The one who hired Valentine? It was Firelight."

Comet and Jason sat cross-legged on the cave floor. Shaggy gave them space so the two of them could hash it out. The floor was cool and soft with dirt fallen from the cave ceiling. Comet could have lain in it and slept a thousand years, he was that tired. "What should I call you?"

"Jason."

"But that ain't your name."

"JT."

"What's it stand for?"

"Nothing. Gene-donors J and T. Embryo 1138. Could have been worse. Could have been donors E-W or P-P or something."

"Genetic experiments?"

Jason shrugged as if the details of his inception and birth didn't matter.

"Is that why the fake ID?"

"No. The fake ID was because I was running away."

"From Valentine?"

"No." Jason glanced over to the sleeping elf. "From everything."

Jason took a deep breath and told Comet the story of how this had all started two years ago when he, Austin, and Austin's sister, Roan, had learned that the rumors surrounding a wizard named Firelight were true: the wizard was capturing kids—orc and elf children and teens, street kids mostly who wouldn't be missed—and doing what with them . . . no one knew, but nothing good. So this was their chance to do the right thing: they'd break Firelight's kidnapping ring wide open. All they needed was proof, and the proof lay in a private med center in Hunter's Point.

Jason called it The Job That Went Bad.

Roan had died, her brain fried by network defenses, and they'd lost Grayson too, the fourth member of their team. And Comet knew how that felt. He'd lost teammates too. But he said nothing because this was Jason's story.

Jason and Austin had been arrested, or so they'd thought until they awoke in an old-fashioned dungeon and not in an SFPD or PBI holding cell. He didn't tell Comet what had been done to them while they'd been prisoners, and Comet knew better than to ask. But the ones who had captured them had been a cabal of wizards called the Thousand Suns, named for the number of stars listed by Ptolemy. Their archmagus was Firelight.

They were Firelight's prisoners for six weeks, and then something happened, Jason didn't know what exactly. Another raid on the facility? An earthquake? For all Jason knew, it could have been The Bomb. But something had set off the alarms and sprang the cell doors and threw the place into chaos, and he and Austin had escaped.

They'd hidden for a while until it all blew over. And then Jason had decided he'd had enough. That was how he'd put it: "I'd had enough." He never told Comet enough of what. And Comet left that alone too, and didn't ask.

He'd contacted Buzz, and Buzz forged the Jason Taylor ID and Jason Taylor moved to the promised land of the orcs—Greentown, Arizona—for a chance to start over. And Comet understood *that* idea perfectly well too, because he'd done the same thing after he'd left the service. And there Jason had met Comet and Duke at a corner table in a dive bar.

"Why didn't you tell me?" Comet asked, because all of Jason's story (still unable to call him JT) was his story too, and if Jason had only told him, Comet would have understood better than anyone.

"I wanted to. I really wanted to. But I didn't want to be JT anymore. I didn't want you to look at me and see two people. I just wanted to be Jason. I just wanted to build fucking cars." He sniffed as if fighting back tears, and the sparks in his eyes swirled brighter. Comet had never seen Jason's eyes fleck with fire outside of sex. He'd never seen Jason so upset as he was now, and he didn't know what to say or do to help him.

"But Firelight's found us again and everything's ruined now. Valentine broke through my firewalls in Greentown. I think she used a vulnerability in some system Dante was jacked into, I dunno. All the alarms went off, and Austin and I ran to help her, but she was already down—" He choked up a bit and wiped his eyes. "We fought our way out, but we couldn't go to a hospital. It was too dangerous. What if Valentine attacked the hospital—could you even imagine? And how would we explain what happened? But Austin said Grandfather Henry could fix her, so we drove here. But Urushiol said that Henry was gone. We went to his house, and it was just like he'd left it for a weekend or something. All his stuff was still there, and Austin found the unicorn horn and stole it. I don't think Urushiol knows we have it. I don't think it'd be very happy if it knew. But Austin said he could use it to fix Dante on his own and we wouldn't need Grandfather to cast the spell. It's some kind of shared dream they're having. He has to convince her to wake up."

"That's not how comas work."

Jason shrugged. "That's how magic works."

They sat quietly awhile and watched the leaves spin in their vortex. Comet didn't understand any of it. Cupid had been their wizard in Reindeer Squad, and Comet had never learned magic. Near the entrance, politely out of earshot, Shaggy watched them patiently. Comet was still linked to him, though they'd not sent to one another in a while. He liked the feeling of Shaggy there, the soft pressure of Shaggy against him like a gaze, like knowing Shaggy wore his clothes.

Jason fidgeted as time passed. He fidgeted the way that experienced drone pilots fidgeted: by moving his drone. He scratched idly at the ground using its clawed foot.

It reminded Comet of the footage Shaggy had recovered: Jason taking down one of Valentine's Ataris with a pack of utility drones like this one. And the soldier in him had to ask: "Just how good are you?"

"You see? That's exactly the kind of thing I was afraid you'd ask if you knew."

CHAPTER ELEVEN

Buzz sat at the cavern entrance and pretended not to hear, but of course he heard everything. And it was hard watching JT tear up, not only because it was always hard to watch a friend hurt, but because JT had left out the part where all this had been Buzz's fault.

It had been Buzz's decision to steal the Blue Unicorn from the Electric Dragon Triad, and then JT and Austin had had to save him from their retribution. And that girl there, Dante, she was hurt because of Buzz. And Buzz didn't want to tell JT what would happen if Austin's spell didn't work, because Buzz knew exactly what would happen: She'd stay in her coma and doctors would try to do their thing, though there was nothing they *could* do, and JT would wear himself down to a ghost with worry and self-hate, and Buzz would walk away scot-free, not a single damn scratch on him when it should have been him lying there.

He'd been arrogant to think he could walk around awake and free and no one would care. Stinking selfish. If he'd been in High Castle with BangBang and Critter and C#Minor, none of this would ever have happened.

JT and Comet sat quietly now, watching the lovely swirl of magic. And he'd have been lying if he'd said there wasn't a jealous stab seeing the two of them together. That was who Comet deserved. Someone like JT, who was strong and smart and wasn't Buzz.

Buzz looked away. The passage outside had a bend to it, and all he could see was a dim glow. He half expected to see BangBang there, hands shoved deep in his pockets, looking forlorn and abandoned and saying, *You promised me you'd come to High Castle.* But of course there was no network here and no BangBang.

The air smelled strange, and for a moment he thought it was BangBang and his stupid cigarettes.

Comet said, "I smell smoke."

The forest itself blocked the view, but to the north, Buzz saw a perfect blue sky filling with gray plumes. They couldn't see flames. To the west, storm clouds gathered: a druidic response to a forest fire. Comet and JT joined him and watched the fire spread.

And of course they all thought of Firelight, but Comet said, "We need to know for sure it's him. I'll go."

He was off in a sprint before anyone could say no.

JT turned away. "Let's get inside."

Buzz didn't want to lose contact with Comet. "No. The cave's too deep. It'll interfere with his signal. Someone needs to stay out here." —*Comet, link your vision.* And Comet did. It was startling how fast the guy could run. Trees whipped by in a blur.

He hated seeing this way. It was always the problem in simflicks too: the actor never looked the same direction you wanted to. They never seemed to focus on the things you were interested in. You knew a good simflick actor and director because they always focused on the things you wanted to see or hear or touch. Comet didn't do that.

—*Stop, goddamn it, stop. What is all that shit?* There were things hanging in the trees, what he couldn't quite tell.

—*Fetishes.* Comet sent, but didn't stop. —*They're all over Arunachal Pradesh these days.*

Even outside, Comet's signal degraded quickly as he passed behind hills and ridges. Comet's feed hung and then jumped to a completely different arrangement of trees and then hung again. —*This ain't a satellite link. Watch your z.*

—*Buzz, you ain't gonna get a clear feed <static> the way it works.*

—*You're getting out of range.*

—*<Static> I'll <static> —ty minutes. Don't <static> —y.*

And their connection dropped entirely.

Buzz paced.

The smell of smoke intensified and the air grew hazy. Buzz could feel it in his lungs.

Comet reconnected and dropped, reconnected and dropped. Through Comet's eyes, Buzz saw smoke and flames, thick and black. He saw something move quickly past his vision, immense. He heard a noise like a growl or a rattle. He caught fragments of sendings from Comet, single syllables. And if one of those syllables had been Buzz's name, that would have been something. But mostly he saw static and heard nothing at all.

JT came outside the cave and watched him pace. Finally he sighed, "Goddess, Buzz. Sit down."

"No."

"Come here and watch this."

Buzz sighed and followed JT inside. He hadn't gotten anything but static and silence for several minutes now anyway. JT put his hand into the magic surrounding Austin and Dante. His touch rippled through it like JT had touched water, rings expanding all the way around and back upon themselves, and the oak leaves went wild. He cringed and went glassy-eyed a moment and then blinked his eyes. "If you touch it, it's like it pulls you halfway into the spell. You can see Dante's dreams."

"What did you see?"

"Dante hates Austin. She thinks he's trying to ruin my life. I told him I should be the one to talk to her, but he said my implants would mess up the spell. So he keeps trying to talk to her and she just runs away. I tried to talk to her myself, but she can't hear me."

"I don't think you should do that anymore." And Buzz went back to pacing.

"He'll be all right."

Buzz knew he meant Comet, not Austin. "You don't know that."

"He's Comet."

"Have you met him? He's completely helpless unless he's got someone telling him what to do! He's . . . he's . . ." and Buzz had no idea what he meant to say next, but his heart was pounding and it had been twenty minutes and Comet should have been back by now.

"Sweet Diana, you're in love with him."

"No," Buzz said. "No, I told you he held a fucking gun to my head. Look!" And he pointed to the tiny, barely existing bruise under his chin. "And then he saved my life, or I saved his, or maybe both, I dunno, but then he handcuffed me to his bed and took his shirt off, and then I got shot and he kissed me—different bed, there were two beds—and Valentine wanted my brain, but he wouldn't give it to her even though he could have, and then he was jumping on cars and almost got himself killed, and I had to drive his damn bike through a fucking car-nado, and I thought he was going to kill us both with a land mine, but he didn't. He held my hand, and we flew just like Kal-El and Lois—I was Lois, he was Kal-El—and we landed and we laughed, and I thought he was going to . . . I wanted him to . . ."

And anyway, if it was love, shouldn't it have felt different? Happy, maybe? Just a *little bit* happy? Not this gut-wrenching thing that made Buzz want to puke up.

"That's gotta be some kind of record." Buzz couldn't tell if JT was pissed or just being sarcastic. "You went from gun to the head to falling in love in what? Six hours?"

"And now he's out there, and God knows what's going on, and you want me to stand here?"

"He's a professional soldier. You're a hacker with a pistol you barely know how to shoot. How are you going to help him?" And JT moved his utility drone between Buzz and the passage outside.

Buzz's glance flicked to the magical vortex. The rings JT had stirred up were gone. "You're right. You're right." And he forced himself to walk away from the passage and over to Austin and Dante. He forced himself to sit when all he wanted to do was run.

JT sat beside him. "He's not an easy person to love."

Yeah? Well, Buzz already fucking knew that, didn't he? He'd had six of hours of intensive training in that. "How long is this spell supposed to take?"

"I dunno. They've been in it forever."

"We can see what they see? All right, let's try it. Maybe there's a way we can help."

So they reached their hands toward the maelstrom, and JT counted down, three, two, one, go, and they touched it.

Except Buzz didn't. And when JT went glassy-eyed, filled with his apprentice's dreams, Buzz ran.

These were a druid's woods. The boles of trees wore faces knotted and creased in bark. Strange fetishes hung from their branches: bits of twig and bone and feathers and fur bound up in hemp string. A light breeze made them spin. They threw leaf-scattered shadows on the pine-needled ground that didn't match their shapes. The shadows were somehow bigger, more solid than the objects that cast them.

JT's bitching and pleading —*That was a dick move, Buzz! You little fucker, get back here! Gods damn you! Please?* came over their network. Buzz ignored him.

He replayed the images Comet had seen when he'd left the cave, and matched them to those he saw now and was able to follow his path, at least until the point where Comet's transmission had failed and what then?

That point came soon enough (and he couldn't hear JT anymore), and he found himself at the base of a ridge with no idea where to go.

Comet's mission had been to scout, wasn't it? So he'd find high ground, wouldn't he? So Buzz climbed to the top of the ridge, but what he found wasn't Comet.

He found a ring of standing stones in a clearing. The stones weren't water-saw-cut like modern stones. These were worn and carved with Celtic knots and serpents and some language he didn't know, and the knots tangled and untangled and the words within their borders crept across the stones. These stones were ancient, non-native, carried from somewhere. He imagined a tanker ship filled with excelsior-packed stone, or airlifted on poly nets across the Atlantic, a caravan of one hundred sixty-five choppers like they were carrying magical nukes. Or maybe they were summoned straight out of the earth and the writing he saw was the words of old gods. Buzz would believe that.

And look at the bones and the blood. My God, it was everywhere. How many people had died here?

The stink of rotting meat was overwhelming. Broken human bones made a carpet. Tarnished chrome and bent steel embellished it.

It was a cybernetic graveyard. He supposed that made sense. The druids would choose modified people as their sacrifices. People like himself and Jason and Comet.

He backed away from the horror of it. Wind gusted. The fetishes clicked and rattled and threw their strange shadows. Those shadows folded and twisted and stood and surrounded him.

They were the wicker creatures he'd seen before: woodwoses. He screamed for help and tried to run, but they caught him easily and lifted him into the air kicking and screaming, and they shoved him into the chest cavity of a wicker giant and the chest closed around him.

He kicked and tore at the straps of wood and shouted "Comet! Comet!" and sent, —*Comet! JT!* But got no reply.

The giant started to walk. It carried him down the hill and into the woods toward the fire in the distance. He'd heard stories of cultists reviving old traditions, and there'd been rumors of burning sacrifices trapped in wicker men.

Maybe the fires weren't Firelight at all, but the druids themselves, and the wooden giant was going to walk right into it, and Buzz would be burned alive.

But that didn't happen.

The base of an immense oak tree had a pit beneath its bole black as pitch. And Buzz, whose Irishness extended no further than his hair color and freckles, still thought of old sidhe and faerie mounds, and the sight of that pit struck a fear in him far disproportionate to what it ought.

The woodwoses threw him into it.

He crashed through mossy roots and clawed out to stop his fall but got no purchase. He hit bottom with a *whump*, unhurt because so much of the forest's debris had fallen through also. The tiny cave wasn't big around, but it was deep. The hole above was just a couple of meters across, if even that, but a full twenty meters up.

Stars cleared from his eyes, and he caught the wind back in him. His eyes adjusted to the darkness, and when he looked up, spitting autumnal debris from his mouth and tasting dirt, he saw Comet.

Roots and vines held him, transfixed, spread-eagled to the wall of the oubliette. So many vines wrapped his arms that, even with his modified strength, he couldn't move at all. Sunlight from above cast a small oval across him. Buzz could see that oval of light move. He could see the shadows over Comet's body shift. Comet breathed heavy and muscles bunched and his veins bulged and he barely moved a millimeter.

The sun would move quickly, then it would be dark here. Utterly dark.

Buzz scrambled over to him and tried to grab hold of some of those vines that wrapped him, to give Comet a fighting chance, but more thin strong roots sprang from the ground and tangled Buzz's feet and drew his wrists back behind him and Buzz fell face-first into the cool rotting loam.

He kept trying. He turned himself around and sat so his fingers could get to the roots that bound Comet's ankles to the wall, but he couldn't get a good grip, and backward like he was, he couldn't get any leverage either. It was the wrong angle for everything.

He struggled against the wall and stood. He attacked the vines at Comet's wrists with his teeth. He tore away bits and pieces and spat them out, but the roots and vines were too thick and Buzz's teeth were only human and not meant for chewing through wood. But he was fuming mad now, and he attacked the roots harder, like he was rabid and crazed, and Comet said, "Buzz. Buzz, it's okay. You ain't a beaver. It's okay."

Buzz yanked hard and his teeth slipped and he fell backward, and pain shot through his mouth, and he landed on his ass in the loam. "It's not okay. We're here! We killed Valentine! It was all supposed to be over! They're gonna kill us, don't you know that? They're gonna burn us in a wicker man, or cut our hearts out on some freaky altar. It's not okay!"

He sat there trying to catch his breath. He prodded at his teeth with his tongue to see if he'd broken anything—no, nothing. His eyes blurred from frustration. Comet glowed through the haze. Comet hung on the wall in his little spot of sunlight bound by stupid plants. They were only stupid plants! And there was nothing Buzz could do. He wasn't strong like Comet was. He wasn't resilient or fast or anything. And all this was his fault anyway. If he hadn't stolen the Blue Unicorn to begin with, none of this would have happened. Comet wouldn't be here, hurt and waiting to die.

Buzz would never have met him.

The angle of the sunlight was sharp. As Comet breathed, shadows thrown by the cobbling of muscle on him went short and long, short and long.

And Buzz remembered JT on a San Francisco rooftop and something he'd said about priorities when you're about to die.

So he crawled back over to Comet, and there was his big-ass belt buckle. For a big-ass belt buckle made to be gaudy, it wasn't all that bad. Buzz caught the edge of it with his teeth and gave it a tug and the buckle popped free.

"What do you need my belt for?" Comet said.

Buzz caught the leather loop in his teeth and pulled and shook his head like he was a dog on a bone. The rich taste of leather filled his mouth, reminding him he hadn't eaten in a really long time, and his mouth went watery.

"You got an idea?" Comet said.

Oh, Buzz had an idea, all right.

He finally got the belt open and it hung there, buckle to one side, loose strap to the other.

Comet's jeans were button-up. Buzz took the corner above the top button in his mouth. The jeans were poly-cotton and the synthetic fibers felt just like real cloth on his tongue. His nose bushed Comet's stomach. It felt like he'd nudged a statue. He popped the button.

Comet said, "Oh."

And what if Comet told him no, what would he do then? But Comet didn't, and Buzz took another mouthful of cloth and freed four buttons *pop-pop-pop-pop* softly, and it was a good thing Comet wasn't wearing no boxers or anything because this here, Buzz wasn't going to be denied this at least. Maybe his teeth couldn't tear through wood, but he'd have eaten right through a pair of boxers if he had to.

He sat back on his bound heels. The dark of Comet's jeans made a V and the hem of his T-shirt made it into a triangle and the top of the triangle was filled with thick short hair that curled like flames, the coloration like everywhere all over his body, and Buzz could see the thick root of Comet's cock.

Of course Comet was thick and of course Comet was a shower and the rest of his cock was still tucked in his jeans. Buzz dug his tongue under Comet's cock, the bit of it he could get to, and sucked and burrowed into the cloth and Comet's crotch like some wild animal burrowing. Comet tasted clean-sweat tangy. Sucking, Buzz tried to pull Comet free, and he came free a little bit, but Comet was starting to go hard. If Buzz didn't free that cock soon, Comet would go really hard, and then Buzz would just have to suck him through the cloth, and that wouldn't be as good as what he intended to do. He tugged on the jeans with his teeth but the jeans were too tight and that got him nowhere, so he said out loud, "Sorry," then bit down on the loose skin and pulled.

"Ow!"

But if the bite had hurt Comet, his cock didn't show it. It went stiff as steel, free.

Buzz nuzzled beneath it, felt the weight of it across his cheek, the smoothness as he turned his head, and Comet hissed from the brush of sideburn along him. Buzz tongued Comet's nuts, still trapped in the jeans, and he tried to work them free the same as he'd done the guy's cock. When he finally gave up and took Comet's sac by the teeth and tugged it free, Comet didn't say ow. He just sighed like it was a relief.

Buzz had been afraid Comet would have one of those crazy-modded cocks—Duke had seemed the kind of guy who'd go for that—but he didn't. He wasn't too far outside of average. It could have been natural. It could have been what he'd started with, only rebuilt. It was thick and just nudged at long-ish. He was uncut. The foreskin wrapped tight and thin. The very tip of his head peeked out, the color of fresh rust. The head was thick like the rest of him, no taper at all, and Buzz thought, *Battering ram*, because he'd read that somewhere, some bit of 1980s imagery passed down a hundred years from sleezy book to sleezy vid to sleezy sim to Buzz right now.

Buzz's wrists dug into vines as he tried to reach for Comet, forgetting for a moment he was as bound as Comet was. He'd have to do this all with his mouth.

He kissed alongside the root of Comet and buried his nose into hair that chemical dyes had made soft. He took a good whiff and thought, *That's Comet's smell, remember that*, all acid and zing. Then he traced the length of him slowly, the gentle zigzags of veins down the right side of him, retracing and memorizing. Same to the bottom of him, the thick ridge of his half-buried urethra. Same on the left, and all the while Comet's cock jumped and flinched and Comet's foreskin retracted millimeter by millimeter until it seemed to catch on the flare of his head and wouldn't draw back any farther. Buzz flicked it free with his tongue, and it settled to where it was supposed to be.

There was pre-come beading. Buzz touched his tongue to it, then pulled away and let the wet string glisten between them like a bridge, like a network cable jacking them together.

Comet's blue glowing eyes closed to mere slits.

Buzz opened wide and exhaled hot air over him before closing his mouth around Comet slowly until his lips touched cock and his tongue touched head. He set to bathing it with his spit, washing it, rolling it, pressing it against the roof of his mouth so when he rolled his head one way, he could tongue him the other, and vice versa. And when his mouth was good and full of his own spit and Comet's pre-come, he pushed himself farther down on him until Comet hit the back of his throat.

And it was like Duke had measured Buzz's mouth and built Comet's cock to fill it and then just a bit more. Like Duke had said Buzz had to work for it and deserve it.

Buzz's tongue was pressed down flat. His jaw was already aching. He couldn't fuck himself on Comet. He couldn't move his tongue the way he wanted, and he tried to shift his angle to something more comfortable. He also fought at the viny bonds at his wrists because, damn it, he wanted to hold onto Comet. He wanted to hold his balls and hold those legs (muscles straining), or grab hold of that ass that tightened and twitched.

He wanted something to hold onto when he took Comet deep.

He looked up at Comet while he sucked him, while the burn of his jaw went hot. And he couldn't tell what Comet was looking at through those monochrome blues: escape, far wall, or Buzz sucking him.

And he tried to figure what kind of guy Comet was, 'cause some guys, they liked it when you choked on their dicks, and some guys, they liked it when your eyes went beet red and the tears streamed. And some liked it better when you took it all without any show at all, like you were meant for them.

Well, he was meant for Comet, wasn't he? He took Comet deep and let Comet's head rest against the back of his throat, soft against soft. He relaxed best he could and pressed on down best he could until that thick head popped on through, his throat open wide, a bit of an ache like when you swallow too big (well, yeah, exactly like that), and kept pressing farther because that was the ache he wanted. His nose finally buried in flame-colored hair, and his chin nestled into the soft tight sack of his nuts, and Buzz was home. Cock halfway to his gut, stretching, the pop of cartilage or something, he didn't know.

This was Comet he had in him.

And Comet said, "Ah fuck, Shaggy. Ah fuck, baby. Fuck."

Shaggy alone would have made Buzz laugh. Except more than that, no one had ever called Buzz *baby* before. No one had ever called him any pet name, and he wondered if Comet called everyone *baby*. He would have smiled if his mouth weren't full of cock. But he couldn't, so he went back to sucking. He pulled himself free and then took it all again and again, enjoying the punch of Comet's head to the back of his throat and the deep sore stretching. He caught breaths when he could, and his neck went sore and his jaw went numb, and Comet was trying to fuck his hips forward but he could hardly move, and he cursed the vines that held him tight and kept saying, "Shaggy, baby."

Buzz made it wet and noisy. He made it messy. Spit dribbled down his chin and stuck to Comet's balls and made sloppy loops that broke against Comet's folded-back jeans and Buzz's T-shirt.

"Shaggy, kiss me. Stop and kiss me."

Buzz didn't want to stop. He wanted to watch Comet writhe in the vines like he was doing. He wanted to hear Comet cuss and beg, because no one had ever begged Buzz for anything before, and he liked it. He liked it especially from this guy here.

"Fucking vines. Fucking druids!" Comet said.

Buzz barely heard him. All he could hear was the churning of spit and pre-come.

What kind of guy was Comet? Did he like to watch himself spray a guy's face, watch it liquefy, run and hang in heavy drops? Did he like to come deep so it wasn't even swallowing, no choice at all? Did he like to shoot in the mouth, a race: can you swallow as fast as I can fill you, or will you overflow? Was Comet's come even come, because Duke could have made it anything. What did it taste like? Had Duke chosen that too?

Comet said, "I'm shooting." And his cock spasmed dry a couple of times and then came the flood.

It felt like come, thick and runny. It tasted like come, mild, neutral, bitter maybe, salty maybe, something else, no more time for tasting, and Buzz had to swallow or it would overflow. Comet bucked and spat more. He was a racing kind of guy, and this was a race Buzz wanted to lose. He wanted all of the above: he wanted it down his throat, in his mouth, all over him. So he kept fucking himself on Comet, deep and hard and fast, and Comet's cock churned jizz and spit into a froth and spat more and rammed it down his throat with its length and shoved it out of him with its width so it bubbled down the front of him and splattered the ground between them.

Comet came forever, that was what Duke had done to him. And when Comet was done, he hung breathless and dizzy from his viny Saint Andrew's, cock stiff as ever, a dripping foamy mess. Buzz tongued it nice and clean.

Buzz sat on his heels. All the aches rose: his throat, his shoulders, his neck, his jaw. His tongue cramped, finally. He knew it would. He belched, tasted come, and swallowed it back down to where it belonged. He was a mess. He couldn't clean himself off. He didn't want to. He wanted to stay just like this, and when the druid came back and found them like this, well, fuck it too.

"Shaggy, kiss me."

No, that wasn't what he wanted to hear. He didn't want to think there might be more to this than sex. Not now while they waited to be horribly killed. He didn't want Comet to kiss him, not even by way of a thank-you. He wanted to sit here in the dark and enjoy the lingering flavor of him.

"Shaggy? Baby?"

Goddamn it. Why now? Was anything fair?

He fought his way standing, and Comet had the faintest smile and his eyes were a soft glowing blue, and he leaned his head forward a bit, as far as he could, and Buzz met him the rest of the way. They kissed, and Comet licked clean Buzz's nose and lips and chin and filled both their mouths with his taste. Honeydew. That was the other part of him. Could come actually taste like honeydew? And what if Buzz hadn't liked honeydew? What then?

But somehow Duke had made Comet for him.

Comet whispered, "I wish I could hold you."

And against all better judgment, Buzz opened a channel and he spun out a space between them, and he shared the sensations and the response packages, all the sims they needed to sense touches neither of them could give. They kissed in the real world. In the virtual they held one another, and Buzz's head fizzed with a whole new kind of despair he wasn't ready to feel: he was going to lose something he'd only just found.

The roots and vines entrapping them spasmed. From above, more dropped to them and pulled Buzz away. "Comet!"

Comet's bonds unfurled, and he fought like a wolverine but that got him nowhere, until they were both vomited up from the oubliette onto the forest floor. The druid stood there with its birch-tree staff. Beside it stood the wizard Firelight.

Firelight reeked of smoke like the stink that fell over inland California during the dry season, and something chemical like what fell over battlefields. He was dressed in pure melodrama: Robes black, cowl black, and the elaborate and arcane trim lining his clothes with runes was just another black in another texture. His robes burned. Flames licked upward from the hem that dragged the ground and made the leaves he walked upon smolder. They licked up from his daggered sleeves and left holes in the cloth. His hands burned. Skin blackened and went shiny and his nails curled and split. And then the tongues of flame passed to another part of him and left pristine skin and cloth behind like it had all been an illusion. But it wasn't an illusion, and his hands trembled and clenched into fists, and the horrible smell of his own roasted meat lingered.

From within the cowl, more flames. Sparks fell from his parched lips when he spoke: "You promised me the orc and the elf if I stopped burning your forest. What is this?"

"Bait. Means to acquire them. They are friends of the orc."

"That was not our agreement. Where are the orc and the elf?"

"I don't know."

—Did it just lie to him? Shaggy sent.

—Sure did. The two of them lay where they'd fallen disgorged from the oubliette. Shaggy didn't move, just looked up at the two beings looming over them. Comet discretely buttoned himself up and then didn't move either.

"You are lord of these woods. You surely know if there are trespassers."

—So it's on our side?

—I don't think I'd go that far.

"Austin Shea is druid trained. I cannot find him." Urushiol nodded toward Comet and Buzz. "Take them and hold them hostage. Austin and JT will come for them."

Comet felt Shaggy's warm hand take his. But Shaggy hadn't moved. They were still linked, and it was just a simulation.

It wasn't enough. They were free from their bonds now, and if he took Shaggy's hand for real, what could Firelight possibly do to stop him? So he reached out and took it, and though they say there's no difference between a simulated sensation and the real thing, that the distinction is impossible to perceive, Comet knew that wasn't true. Nothing could replace this.

Firelight watched their fingers thread together as if it were some insignificant and impotent reflex, like the dying kick of a bug. "Yes, they will try to save them, won't they."

Urushiol glanced up to the sky. It had darkened with storm clouds and smoke. A heavy drop of rain slapped into the leaves so close to Comet's nose that it splattered him. More drops followed. The druid began to walk away. "Then take them and leave."

"So you can scheme your vengeance against me with Austin Shea, student of your own student, one of your own lineage?"

Urushiol slowed and stopped walking. "Austin Shea is a *failed* student of our path. He is nothing to me. Our business is concluded, yours and mine. Fire is part of the cycle of things. I have no further grievance with you."

Firelight's quivering hands took the edges of his cowl and drew it back. He was a white man. He was bald. Flames ate at his face and scalp and ruined him, and then they vanished and he was repaired. He let the cowl fall to his shoulders.

Across their network, Comet sent a knowing, victorious laugh. —*Get ready to run.*

—*Why are you laughing? This isn't funny. It's scary as hell.*

—*Because he's a dragon's apprentice, and that's a serious fucking character flaw.*

Firelight rolled his head, and his bones popped and began to distend. He said to the druid, "Liar. All things crave vengeance."

CHAPTER TWELVE

irelight erupted into a beast like Comet had only heard of: twelve meters long, most of him tail and neck, a winged *Deinonychus*, some cross between lizard and bat. His arms unfurled into wings with long, elegant, webbed digits, and his legs became thick and powerful with muscle. His head had a mane of feathers and seven rococo horns. His robes were part of his magic, and they became his scales: sleek, oily black, the color car designers wished their black could be, delicately etched with alchemical symbols and flickering with an orange patina like they were on fire. His breath smelled of chemicals and his ragged mouth drooled venom. The claws of one foot, only a meter from Comet and Shaggy, were forty centimeters of steel. He was entirely terrifying and magnificent. Comet could barely breathe and couldn't even blink, he was so beautiful. Firelight had become a drake. And even in all that awe and power, he was still only the pathetic mortal dream of what a true dragon was. That dream was enough.

Urushiol slammed its birch-tree staff down. Briars curled from the ground into thickets. Trees uprooted and formed a phalanx. The storm overhead snapped and threw down bolts of blue lightning with deafening booms. Comet's ear canals narrowed to filter the sound, eyes polarized against the flash. Clean ozone and weird static zinged in the air.

Firelight the drake leapt at the phalanx of trees protecting the druid and tore with his great steel claws.

Comet had never fought a wizard, not face-to-face. Cupid had been their wizard in Reindeer Squad, and he'd been a guards-and-wards magus, not the blow-em-up kind, and he certainly couldn't change his shape. Comet (like most people) had the sense that true wizards were immortal. Cupid hadn't been immortal, but he hadn't been easily killed either. His death had been long and terrible, and Comet had been unable to stop it. Comet had no idea how to fight this wizard.

—Run! Don't let go! Don't look back! as if they were Lot's wife escaping Sodom, or Orpheus tempted by Eurydice's silence, or Indy and Marion averting their eyes from the Ark. The two beings battling behind them were nearly gods, Kong vs Godzilla.

Comet ran over the top of the druid's briar and hauled Shaggy up a tree, hoping it wouldn't start moving at the druid's command.

—On my back! Comet sent, and some twenty yards up in the air, balanced on a tree bough barely half a meter across, Shaggy trusted him utterly and leapt on his back. Comet smiled, saying to himself, *I've won him,* because the Shaggy of eight hours ago would never have done what he'd done just now. Shaggy's arms went around his neck, and Comet caught his legs in his arms, and he ran.

Shaggy weighed 60 kilos, just a slip of a guy to Comet, who could lift a car if he tried.

—Where are we going?

—Away from JT and his friends.

—He'll catch us. It'll be just like Urushiol said. He'll use us as bait.

—I know.

The drake's head snapped their direction and screeched with eagle-like hate. He abandoned his assault on the druid and leapt into the air after them. But the forest was dense, and the druid's magic spurred its wild growth, and Firelight was simply too big. His wings battered against branch and bole, and he fell. He tried again and again. He scraped and clawed against the trees and tore their strange face-like bark to shreds. Fetishes caught in his horns and began to smolder.

Comet ran. He ran the length of one branch, leapt to another and then to a third. His muscles screamed and reminded him it had been only two hours since he'd fallen off a car and hit pavement at 150 KPH. And 60 kilos had felt like nothing for a few of those amazing leaps, but Shaggy was starting to feel a whole lot heavier now.

His body pumped him full of endorphins and painkillers and his implants made him feel like a million bucks, all of it a lie. He dialed back the pain-dampening so he had a better sense of when his body would give out, and the sudden overwhelming ache of everything made him slip, and Shaggy yelped in terror before Comet managed to steady himself.

So much for that idea, and he turned the pain-dampening all the way up. He'd drop dead from exertion and never know it was coming.

—What are you doing to yourself?

Comet had forgotten Shaggy had access to Comet's life monitors.

—You can't do that.

—I know what I'm doing.

—Bullshit you do. Stop it. Stop it or I'll let go.

—You let go, you fall.

Shaggy cussed him, but Comet didn't care. He ran his crazy Tarzan run, the worst obstacle course of his life. He could keep this up for three minutes? Five? Then they'd have to turn and fight and what would he do then? Surrender? That idea galled, but he'd do it. He'd do it if that meant Shaggy lived even one hour longer.

And below them, threading the forest floor, constantly hampered by trees and thorns, Firelight tried to run, tried to fly, and finally, driven to madness by the two men scampering through the trees just out of his reach, he spat his venom into the forest and ignited it.

Firelight Who Had Stood in the Maw of Abbadon the Red, Was Consumed, and Reborn spat a stream of viscous poison and spoke the words to ignite it: a hundred names he knew for fire: Fire. Fuego. Feuer. Fogo. Foc. Fuoco. Brasa. Вогонь. Агонь. Yangın.

Below Comet and Shaggy, orange bloomed from the drake's distended jaws. Comet jumped blind. Fire engulfed everything where they had stood. Heat blasted him. His thermal-sensitive hair went white. His mechanical eyes filtered the sudden flare. The air expanded like a concussion grenade had gone off and blew him even farther than he'd jumped. Shaggy lost his grip and flew from him.

He lashed out and caught Shaggy by the arm with one hand and branch after branch with the other, trying to slow their fall without dislocating Shaggy's shoulder in the process. But it was a crazy fall, and there was no skill to this, no *qīnggōng* here, just desperation. Tree limbs battered them, but slowed them with every snag and tear. Above him, the forest canopy went up in an inferno.

They hit the ground badly, and lost precious moments while Shaggy fought to stand with the breath knocked clean out of him.

The rain came down hard now, Urushiol trying to save his Devastation forest. The air was gray with it. Their hair was plastered and in their eyes, and still the canopy above them burned as if no amount of water could drown the drake's fury.

Between the rain and the fires overhead, Comet's thermal vision was fucked, and he couldn't see Firelight anymore. How could anyone lose something so big?

—*Keep running. Come on, Shaggy, keep running.*

Comet had carried Buzz like he was a fucking baby. He was less than useless. He was a liability. He was gonna get Comet killed. He was gonna get JT killed, and Austin killed, and Dante killed. Dante, who hadn't done anything to anyone except be in the wrong place at the wrong time. Hurt now and in a coma for no more reason than because the Blue Unicorn had spoken to her: *"Help me, Dante Riggs."*

And fuck that thing. Fuck the Blue Unicorn! He wished he'd never saved it. It wasn't even a person, not even an AI. It was just a bundle of memories strung together and replaying obsessively, memories that just happened to belong to an old dead friend that he missed terribly.

Buzz ran through the deluge and beneath spreading flames. He slipped on wet needles and mud. His hand left Comet's, and he was afraid Comet would leave him, but he didn't. Of course he didn't. Comet stopped, and they took each other's hand again and kept running (Comet running so much slower than he could have, all because of Buzz).

A wizard could be killed. Austin had done it not two days before. He'd burned a necromancer made of hell money and the necromancer's spirit had returned to its rest. There was a trick to killing one: the closing of a circle of metaphors. Buzz wasn't a mystic. He didn't understand these things. Metaphors were for English majors, and he'd never even gone to college.

And maybe Buzz didn't understand it quite right, but he knew this: Firelight was evil. Wholly evil in every way there was. And Firelight had sought the AI ghost who called herself the Blue Unicorn, after one of the purest creatures ever imagined, one murdered for its horn years ago. And that very horn lay in a cave in Austin's hand. If ever there was a chain of metaphors and meanings that should have been magical, this was it.

—*The unicorn horn can kill him.*

Comet didn't question him, not even a moment. They changed directions and ran for the cave.

Near the cave, they both hammered the network hoping JT would hear: —*JT! JT! He's coming! Firelight's coming! Fire up that drone! Give it a gun! He's coming!*

Through the gray of the rain, Buzz barely saw anything, but heard the eagle-like shrieks behind them growing nearer. Then they burst into the cave, stumbling, drenched, water streaming from their hair (Comet's cool and red now).

The ground shook and dirt fell in little rivulets from the cave ceiling.

"Get back. Get back!" Comet shoved Buzz behind him and drew his pistol. Buzz stood behind him but pulled his too.

—*JT, we need the horn!*

—*No! Austin needs it for the spell!*

Firelight, human so as to fit through the cave's mouth, appeared in a swirl of flame. No one hesitated. Everyone fired: Comet with his pistol. Buzz with Comet's spare (recoil painful as ever). JT's little drone with an assault rifle taped to it jury-rigged. JT himself stood guard over the two sleepers as if his body could stop the wizard's approach.

The wizard swept bullets away with his hand. Some struck him anyway, tiny violent explosions of black cloth as they tore into the wizard's body and appeared to do nothing but enrage him further. He transformed right before them, and there was the drake. His black scales gathered the strange light of Austin's spell. He blocked the exit. He was huge and only showed how large the cave was by the fact he didn't fill it.

Firelight didn't bother to deflect the bullets now. They sparked and ricocheted off the impenetrable scales of the thing, but the bullets must have stung because his jaws spread wide and he spewed his venom and spoke his words, and fire engulfed JT's drone. He kept on, more and more flame, until the drone glowed like the nose of an orbital plane on re-entry. When the drake stopped breathing, the drone slumped, waxenly formless.

—JT, the horn!

—No!

Comet shot Buzz a glance. Buzz ran for the whirlwind spell and the horn that powered it.

Comet ran out of ammo, dug in his pockets for more, and came up empty-handed. He dropped his pistol and charged the drake. He fucking charged him, like he was going to beat him senseless with his damn hands! Buzz stopped, frozen solid with fear for Comet.

Comet leapt and kicked the thing so hard in the chest, Firelight stumbled back—just one hind foot repositioned, but still, he stepped back. His jaw snapped at Comet, so he whirled and kicked him in the chin. Firelight roared, and fire ran from the corners of his mouth. *—Shaggy, I ain't doing this to look good!*

"No, Buzz! Please, she'll die!" JT moved to intercept him like this was a football game.

—He'll kill us all, JT, and Buzz tried to slip past him.

JT made a half-hearted swipe to stop him. One last feeble, *—Please, Buzz, don't,* and he caught Buzz by the jacket. Buzz thought it was all over. There was no way he could wrestle free of an orc, but then JT let him go.

Buzz fell into the spell, and its magic pulled weirdly at what little aura remained to him. He reached for the horn, and Austin's spell sucked him in.

There's a million kilometers of road ahead, all arrow straight. She's got her truck (monster wheels one K high); she's got a friend (the name is a blur in her head and she can't pin it down, but her friend don't seem to mind); and it's a beautiful fucking day (sky the color of a sim with no feed: Bill Gates's blue). Dante rolls down the windows. The wind smells like cookies.

She's headed West—capital W-e-s-t—where Elrond and Gandalf and Frodo went. It's somewhere near Hawaii, she thinks.

She feeds music into the truck. "'It's a death trap. It's a suicide rap. You better get out while you can.'" Crap music. It's not part of her collection. She don't know where it came from.

Her friend says something. Dante don't know what. (She hasn't made any sense yet.) Her friend says: AC23:A0CE:9292: 1B60:2001:2010:2061:3001.

There's a hitchhiker on the side of the road dressed in Vietnam camo. Elf ears stick through cuts in his floppy fisherman's hat. He tries to wave her down, fucking loser. He's been trying to wave her down since forever.

Dante, can you hear me? It's Buzz, do you know me? You need to stop for him. He's trying to help. But Dante won't hear him, and Dante doesn't stop.

Dante Riggs has got her road. She's got her truck. She's got a friend. There's nothing else she wants. Dante Riggs will drive West forever. There's a million K of road ahead. And each K a hitchhiker, all of them elves, all tragic as fuck.

They pass him again. He holds up a sign. He's held signs before. *Please stop. I'm a friend. Going West.* All lies. The sign he holds now: *JT loves you.*

She don't know what that means, and it makes her so angry. She asks her friend what it means.

Her friend says: 2001. 2010. 2061.

It's 2075, goddamn, don't you know?

So she stops and pops the door. Her friend slides to the middle and the elf climbs in. Her friend says to the elf the first thing she's ever said that makes any sense. She says:

```
printf("hello, world");
```

It was the ancient programmer's mantra that did it, and Buzz broke free of Dante's dream.

The unicorn horn in Austin's hand shone brighter than the Pleiades. Still, it seemed to take years to reach it. But he did. And he turned and threw it toward Comet, a charming and perfectly hopeless throw.

Another roar and a *whump* and it was a good thing Comet couldn't feel a damn thing. Comet flew, swatted through the air by the drake's tail, to slam into an immense hanging root. He fell to the floor, landing on hands and knees, and the drake reared back and inhaled deep.

The whirlwind spell broke apart with a strange slow sigh, and Comet felt the explosion of magical power tug at what little was left of his aura. Firelight felt it fully. The drake's breath hitched. He didn't spray venom and fire as he had meant to.

The unicorn horn tumbled in the air, nowhere close to Comet. Comet almost laughed it was so beautiful that Shaggy couldn't throw for shit.

He leapt and caught the horn in midair, and he sailed across the cave, and anyone who might have seen him would have said he could fly, though that was impossible, wasn't it? He slammed hard into the drake's neck. He wrapped his legs and one arm around him so he couldn't be shaken free, and he drove the tiny horn under Firelight's scales and into flesh. The beast's skin sparked. Silver-white cracks spiraled out from the wound, shattering scale after scale, the cracks like gunshots. Comet stabbed again and again, over and over, and searing blood sprayed everywhere. Comet dove away from the rain of poisonous blood and rolled to safety.

Firelight gurgled his name, lost his form, became a wizard again. He staggered against the wall of the cave entrance, hand against his neck. Between his fingers, blood flowed violently free. He gave them an all-encompassing look of such venomous hate that it froze them in their tracks as if it were a spell. Then he fled out the tunnel and into the woods.

CHAPTER THIRTEEN

They ran down the mountainside. Comet and Shaggy carried a groggy Austin between them, though Comet wasn't doing much better. He slowly dialed back his pain-inhibition and let himself feel the damage one abrasion, cut, bruise, and cracked bone at a time. Jason carried Dante, still as unconscious as ever.

Far away and high above, Firelight flew west. He was barely a speck against the storm raging around him.

They slid down muddied embankments and kept running until the rains let up and the druid's tempest was behind them and there was sunlight again, a different world than the one they'd just left. They'd reached the end of Urushiol's demesne.

Ahead: a ruined blacktop road that hadn't seen traffic in years, except for a 2074 Corvette Dawnstrike FX27 painted Event Horizon Black and a customized Kawasaki crotch-rocket painted Comet-colored. How the motorcycle had gotten there, who could say? The druid, Comet supposed. The hood of the Corvette was banged up all to hell, like a hailstorm or a bag of nails had hit it. The Kawasaki was scratched up and battered too. There were clumps of dirt and grass in the engine and twigs caught in the wheel framing.

Jason laid Dante on the pavement. They all stood around her and waited. Either she'd awaken now, or . . . well, Comet didn't know what. He wasn't a medic or wizard, either one.

Shaggy looked terrible.

—*You okay?* He sent just to Shaggy so no one else heard.

—*I don't think so,* Shaggy sent back.

—*You did the right thing.*

—*I want the right thing to feel like the right thing.*

And he tried to take Shaggy's hand through their link, but Shaggy didn't send the response packages, so Comet stopped trying.

Dante stirred. Her eyes fluttered open, and Jason spoke a prayer of thanks to a goddess he never named, and Austin sighed a nonreligious, "Thank God."

She said, "JT?"

"I'm here."

"JT, they killed a unicorn."

"It was just a dream. Somebody else's dream. It happened a long time ago."

"It felt so real," she said, confused and doubting him.

—See? You did good, Comet sent to Shaggy. *—You saved everybody.*

—Yeah.

Sending was a sensation half between sound and reading, toneless in its way. But Comet knew exactly what Shaggy was feeling. He wanted to be alone, the same way Comet so often felt after something bad was over.

And Comet wanted out of here, he wanted good and gone. He was hurt worse than he'd been hurt in a long time, and it went deeper than bruises or cracked bones. And he could barely look at Shaggy, because what did they do now? Where did they go from here?

Near the Corvette, Shaggy and Austin fussed over Dante. Dante obviously didn't like being fussed over. She kept slapping at Austin.

She said, "Don't start thinking I like you. Don't start thinking I appreciate you running around in my fucking head, because I don't. I'm gonna have bad dreams about elves for a week."

"I saved your goddamn life."

"Yeah, thanks. Except this was all your fault to begin with, so what I really mean is *fuck off.*"

Shaggy said, "Hey, we were just trying to—"

"And you fuck off too. I don't know you from anyone!" She'd come out of her day-long coma confused and clumsy and needing help for everything. She really didn't like that.

Comet and Jason—he still couldn't call him JT—sat on the old battered guardrail overlooking a ravine. Their feet were propped so they looked like gargoyles perching (Jason more so than Comet).

"She ain't very grateful," Comet said.

"Should she be?"

"I suppose not."

"Austin did save her, though," Jason conceded. "To be honest, I didn't think he could do it."

"Why did you let him?"

"I didn't have any choice. I had to trust him. And it worked, and now I feel shitty for not trusting him."

He watched Jason watch Austin. Comet wasn't sure what to think about the elf. The elf was beautiful, sure, but in that dodgy kind of way that made smart people keep their distance. And maybe Jason wasn't all that smart, because there was something between the two of them, Comet could tell. And he thought it was more than just gratitude for saving his protégé's life.

"Are you in love with him?"

"He's an elf. Everybody loves elves. Buzz is in love with you, you know."

And if that wasn't an evasion, Comet didn't know what was. But he let it go. Shaggy was tucking Dante into the back of the car. He covered her with a stolen ambulance blanket. "Is he?"

"You can't tell?"

Shaggy caught Comet looking at him and looked away fast, pretending not to have noticed.

"I'm surprised the two of you aren't off fucking in the woods, what with the way you get after a fight and that boner you're trying to hide."

"Ain't trying to hide anything." He shifted his legs a bit so Jason couldn't see. "We don't need to fuck, we need to talk."

Jason laughed. It wasn't a booming sort of laugh like Duke had. But it was loud and clean, four sharp barks that faded into a snicker and a shake of the head. "So it really is love."

And Comet knew he was trying to make a joke, but the nagging doubt that grew every passing minute Shaggy didn't talk to him made it fall flat. Because he barely knew the guy. They'd known each other eight hours, was all. And maybe this space between them just now was because Shaggy had come to his senses and knew there was no future for a thief and his paladin. Maybe Comet had been wrong, and there'd been nothing between them but two people hopped up on adrenaline and fear and needing a release. It wouldn't be the first time.

Shaggy still refused to look his way.

It was time to go.

"I'll see you in Greentown?"

JT shook his head. "I can't go back. Not until all this is done."

It wasn't what Comet wanted to hear, but he knew it was true, so he nodded once and stood and started for his bike.

And halfway there he slowed and he stopped and he turned, and there was Shaggy watching him go, and Comet couldn't walk away from him. He jerked his head, *C'mon*, for Shaggy to follow.

But Shaggy shook his head no and turned back to the car.

JT took Buzz by the shirt and slammed him into the Corvette. "What the fuck are you doing?"

"I can't go with him. I can't, JT. I can't."

"You're fucking going with him, or I'm fucking tearing your head off." JT's eyes had that worked-up look.

"No, you don't understand." Buzz was nearly in tears.

JT said, "Austin, you got handcuffs?"

"About a dozen." Austin popped the glove compartment and pulled out a pair of cuffs and tossed them to JT. JT yanked Buzz's hands behind his back and wasn't gentle about it at all when he slapped the cuffs on Buzz's wrists.

"This ain't funny, JT! I'll remember this! Goddamn you!"

JT hauled him off to the middle of the road, held up Buzz by the scruff of his shirt so his toes were just grazing the ground, and shouted at Comet, "We ain't got room for this guy. And the way I understand it, he's your prisoner anyway."

He let go, and Buzz's knees cracked into the pavement. Already banged up and scabbed up, he broke into tears from the pain and couldn't cuss JT fast enough or blue enough, so he executed a goddamn program to spam the bastard with curses, net-wise. JT just laughed and blocked him.

The orc went over to the Corvette and climbed in. Austin saluted them all. Then the batwing doors folded gracefully down, and the beautiful car with its beautiful hood damage slid blackly past them out onto the county road no one knew the name of, and was gone. All that was left was Comet and Buzz.

Buzz didn't like the look on Comet's face. Comet looked mean.

Buzz said, "This wasn't my idea. JT was being a jackass. C'mon, let me go."

Comet bent over him and riffled through the pockets of his motorcycle jacket (Comet's motorcycle jacket). He pulled out the little chip, the simple password hacker Buzz had used in Comet's apartment to break free of that first set of cuffs.

"Thanks," Buzz said just a bit too early.

Comet dropped the chip onto the asphalt and slammed his boot down on it. He ground his heel with a crunchy insect sound.

"What the fuck, man!"

Comet threw his leg over his bike and brought it upright under him. "Get on."

"Like this? I can't hold on!"

"Have you ever actually tried to hold on?"

CHAPTER FOURTEEN

Travel Advisory: Comet

Buzz leaned into Comet, cheek against the plastic spinal ridge of his banged-up, shot-up, torn-up jacket. He listened to the screaming wind. It made him think of banshees and dead Irishmen.

At the first working cell-tower:

Buzz stood in the Ultraviolet and watched Breugel's castle grow. He was one of thousands. BangBang and Critter found him, no surprise there. And they stood beside him quietly, which was a surprise.

Bruegel's castle was mathematical. It looked like a castle only because Buzz chose to interpret his old lover's data that way (Breugel had been the one to teach him that). He didn't have to see it that way. His protocol could have interpreted the complex mathematics Bruegel transmitted as anything, even raw data endlessly streaming in alchemical green down his visual field.

Somewhere in all that math dreamt his old lover. Buzz didn't love him anymore. He never had. He'd never been wise enough to know what love was, although he thought he might be now.

Breugel's art unfolded in increasing complexity, proving endless theorems, postulating more. His adherents worshipped him. Their avatars knelt and walked away dazed and enlightened somehow, and Buzz knew this worship, this holy power, was because of him and what he had done. Did anyone know what it had cost him?

Because Breugel had been an abusive fuck as a human, and he didn't deserve any of this, but like everyone abused, Buzz had blamed it on himself and given it to him anyway. This crazy scene here, these digital apostles and their mindless god, just now it felt less like *The Passion of the Christ* and more like *Life of Brian*.

And he imagined Breugel's body, withered and kept alive by chemicals and machines, barely more than a brain in a jar.

And BangBang sent, —*There will always be another Valentine. And the next one will go after the ones you love. And your soldier won't always be there to save you.*

They watched a while longer, time running strangely here, and Buzz hoped his link to the working wireless tower would fail, but it didn't.

—*I know. I'm ready.*

—*You won't regret this, Buzz.*

A new tower sprang from the castle, and Breugel's apostles cheered.

—*That could be you in there,* BangBang sent, and God help him, but he obviously thought that was a good thing.

He wrote Comet a goodbye letter, or that was the intention.

First iteration: —*Had a good time, good luck, and goodbye.* Trite and dishonest.

Second: —*When I first started thinking there might be something to this . . .* but it bogged down in the middle and went on too long.

Third: —*I'm a really bad lay anyway. You wouldn't like me at all.*

Fourth: he added a recording of himself he'd done once to prove he wasn't kidding.

Fifth: He flipped through his porn collection. Somewhere had to be motorcycles. He found one that looked like Comet's. He cracked the copyright protection. He deleted the biker and pasted in a sim he'd done of himself jacking off for an old boyfriend a few years back. At a working wireless tower, he went online and found a jacket that was close enough to the one he was wearing and dressed himself up in it. He repositioned his hand a bit. He added handcuffs. He made the spray of come ridiculous, buckets. He spent a long time on that because spurting fluids were hard to model and get the physics right. The end result was silly. A gag gift. (And he forgot to add the part where he said goodbye.)

Once they got back to Greentown, he'd slip away. He'd send it from the *Marid*. Or maybe he wouldn't, and he'd just leave without a word.

Was he that much of a chickenshit?

Yeah. Yeah, he was.

He hit Send.

He panicked.

Oh God. Oh Christ. What had he been thinking? That bike was Comet's heart and soul. He loved that goddamn thing. And Buzz had sent him a video of himself jizzing all over it? Christ. He broke out in a sweat. His pulse thundered. It was too late now. He waited. He waited and he waited and he waited for Comet to say something. And the longer Comet went without saying something, the more it seemed proof that he'd pissed Comet off.

Kilometers slid by.

Or maybe Buzz was lucky and Comet had been so torqued with him, he had just deleted it unseen? Yeah, that had to be it. Thank God. Thank God.

But then the bike slowed. Comet pulled off to the side of the road, gravel popping under the tires. He said, "Get off the bike."

"Comet, I'm sorry. I didn't—"

"Shut up. I said get off the bike."

Buzz slid off the bike. Handcuffed like he was, he almost fell. Comet didn't help him. Comet was gonna leave him here. Comet wouldn't leave him here, would he?

But Comet kicked the stand down and got off the bike too. He backed off a few meters. He folded his arms on his chest and cocked his head to one side. "Kick your right shoe off."

Buzz just stood there and didn't know what to do.

"Come on. Right shoe."

So Buzz did, and he stood there one bare bloodied sock against the gravel. He started to sweat from the heat. Comet went up to him and pulled him close by the waistband of his jeans (Comet's jeans). Comet unbuttoned them.

"What are you doing? Someone will see." Though they hadn't seen a soul on this road in hours.

"Shut up."

He yanked the jeans and Buzz's boxers down, had Buzz pull his right leg free, and left the jeans tangled around the shoe he still wore. Sunlight hit Buzz's copper bush, and it went bright orange. He wasn't hard. He was half-scared, more than half-embarrassed. He could feel heat in his chest and shoulders and cheeks and ears like the whole top third of his body had caught on fire.

"Lean over my bike," Comet told him. "Like you're gonna get on. There ya go. That's it. Now stop."

And if Buzz had thought he'd been embarrassed before, he was going to die now. His left foot and its tangle of jeans and boxers held him steady. His stomach lay over the engine compartment, its heat warming him to sweat worse. His right leg was tucked under him, shin on the soft seat. In front of him was the right handlebar. He could smell the heat from the engine. He could smell the dirt and sweat left by Comet's hand on the handlebar grip. His shoulders were sore from the cuffs holding his arms back. His wrists were sore too.

And he could feel a breeze on his asshole. It wasn't a place he was used to feeling breezes. He could feel the damp sweat there drying. He could feel his ass hairs shift under the sun.

Buzz wasn't a virgin, but like many net-savvy people, most of his sex had been virtual. He'd simulated all kinds of crazy things, but simulations were porn. They were stylized, edited. The clumsy false starts, the smells, the tastes, the pain, the discomfort afterward, all of that gone or carefully chosen to appeal to certain tastes. Simulations weren't real sex; some didn't even pretend to be. Some critics said simstim had made a whole generation of people who didn't know how to touch another person. Maybe that was true. Buzz liked giving blowjobs, but he could count the guys who'd fucked him on one hand. And Comet scared him.

There was nothing simulated about what Comet was going to do. Right here on the side of the road—Comet's bike rack-like beneath him, Comet's jacket sun-warm on his back, Comet's jeans gathered down around one ankle—Comet was going to fuck him.

Comet came round to the front, where Buzz could see him. Buzz's hair fell in his eyes, so it was hard to see. Comet brushed it out of his way, and the gentle way he tucked his too-long bangs behind his ear, that was when Buzz knew Comet wasn't mad at him. Comet wasn't doing this to embarrass Buzz or punish him. Comet was doing this because he thought it was hot.

"Goddamn, you're beautiful," Comet whispered.

And Buzz thought, *No, please don't do this. Please don't make this any harder than it already is. It was supposed to be a goodbye, not this. Please.*

But he didn't say any of that because if he did, Comet might stop.

Comet had stepped back, and he was looking Buzz up and down. Comet plucked at the hem of his shirt. He shrugged his jacket off, and it fell with a rustle into the roadside weeds, and his black, sleeveless compression T-shirt showed every curve and plane of him shadowed in low angled light. Sunlight caught the bio-engineered dye in his hair, and his colors went rampant. His eyes were cobalt like the sky behind him, like his eyes were cutouts and Buzz could see right through him. He ran a hand over his stomach. And Buzz watched him closely, because the way Comet touched himself, that was the way he liked to be touched, and Buzz would need to know that later. (He tried not to think of later.)

Comet pulled the shirt up, exposing rippling stacks of muscles and the barely existent flame-trail of hair that ran between them. The shirt was so tight it stayed wrapped over his chest, and he flicked at one pale-brown nipple until it went hard and sharp. The amber of his skin, and the flame of his hair, and the blue of his eyes, he was a sun god in the making.

A sun god who'd just had the shit beat out of him. There was barely a centimeter of him that wasn't bruised. That perfect cobblestone stomach was mottled purple and green. He was nicked and cut and bloodied. The rain and wind and dust had turned his hair into a wild matted mass. He looked so awful that Buzz thought, *Maybe now's not a good time. Maybe we shouldn't do this.*

He didn't say that either.

And he could see the thick bar of Comet's cock hanging to the right in his jeans. Comet wanted Buzz. The thought barely made sense to him. The hottest man in the world, the bravest man in the world, the most loyal man in the world wanted everyday, boring Buzz.

This guy punched a dragon and now he's gonna fuck me.

Buzz was plenty hard now.

Comet knelt in front of him so they were eye level to each other. The pupil-less void of Comet's eyes were Buzz's own private eternity. Comet took him by a hank of his dirty, windblown hair and pulled his head back. It stung and Buzz's eyes teared up. Comet leaned in close to Buzz's ear and said, "This is what you get for coming on my bike."

He gave Buzz a wicked smile, stood, unbuttoned his jeans, and worked his thick cock out of them. He let it wag there in front of Buzz, right at mouth level. The head of it was candy red, and the foreskin was drawn full back, and as it wobbled, pre-come beaded at the tip and sagged south. Buzz tried to lick it. Comet kept it just out of reach. Buzz tried to squirm forward, but he was afraid the bike would go over and he'd land face-first in the gravel curb, ass in the air. (And that might not have stopped Comet. He'd have fucked Buzz anyway.)

Comet thumped him on the temple for trying. It wasn't a hard thump, just enough to surprise Buzz and teach him to hold still. Comet wiped the head of his cock across Buzz's nose and left a thick bead of moisture where Buzz couldn't reach with his tongue. He took Buzz by the hair again and slapped his cock against Buzz's cheeks a few times. But he wouldn't put it in Buzz's mouth where Buzz wanted it. "You already got what you wanted out of me. It's my turn. Yeah, I owe you for that too, you smart-mouthed little fucker."

Comet went back around where Buzz couldn't see him, and that was maddening, not knowing where the guy was or what he was planning, so he cheated and accessed the bike's cameras, and through them saw Comet crouched and staring at Buzz's bare ass, balls and cock hanging free, the tip of Buzz's cock pressed by his own hard-on uncomfortably against the bike's engine.

And Comet leaned in close, and Buzz thought of sims again and how he had to smell down there because how long had it been since he'd had a shower?

Comet's tongue met his asshole and Jesus fucking Christ.

Comet's hands spread his ass cheeks, and Buzz felt the hot air of Comet's breath along the hairs there (and his asshole puckered and sucked in and bloomed, and Comet shook his head, smiling), and then the soft warmth of his tongue prodding in, and the burn of whiskers on sensitive skin not used to anything but Charmin. The burn was too much, his ass too tender, not used to this at all. Buzz went to tune the sensation, dull the burn and magnify the flick of Comet's tongue and the strange spreading warmth of Comet forcing spit deep into his ass.

But then he tuned nothing. He filtered nothing, magnified nothing. Comet would take him however Comet wanted, and Buzz would feel all of it.

Buzz made little puff of air noises when the sensation of tongue or teeth surprised him. He gritted his own teeth and whimpered when it started to burn. He forgot to look through the camera. It went on forever. He fought his handcuffs, and the bike wobbled, and he went still. One leg shook; the other went numb.

And then Comet stood, leaned over Buzz, and took Buzz in his arms from behind, and Comet's cock lay right in the crevice of his ass and Christ, it felt big. Ten times bigger than it looked. And Comet's hard body pressed Buzz's hands down on the cuffs so that they hurt, and he wrapped one arm around Buzz's neck and pulled Buzz's head back, turning him for a clumsy kiss. The position was uncomfortable. It hurt his wrists and his shoulders and his neck. He didn't want Comet to ever let go.

"Gonna fuck you now," Comet said.

And Buzz nodded frantically, yes, yes, oh my God, yes.

Then Comet adjusted himself and pressed, and Buzz tightened up like he shouldn't have done, but Comet kept pressing, and Buzz was so slick it popped right in with a sharp stab of pain. Buzz cried out and tried to pull away but Comet held him tight and told him to breathe and push out, push out, breathe and breathe, you can take it.

Comet's entry went on forever. Like there was an infinite amount of him that needed to be in Buzz. And Buzz thought, *He's inside me. Comet's inside me.* And that seemed like the most wonderful impossibility ever there was.

"How you doing?" Comet whispered in his ear.

Buzz couldn't say anything. He could barely focus on anything but Comet's happy smile in the motorcycle's cameras.

Comet had opened that file and watched the vid of Shaggy jizzing onto his bike, and goddamn, that had pissed him off, like Shaggy was mocking him for being naive and loyal and all those things no thief had any concept of. It might as well have been a video of Shaggy jizzing on Comet's face.

Except that thought wasn't so bad. And he'd felt that itch he'd felt every damn time he looked at Shaggy.

He watched the vid again and again, and each time Shaggy came that ridiculous firehose splash all over his bike, it was like Comet could feel it. And he thought, *You little smart-ass fucker. You come on my bike, I'll show you what you get. I'll show you.* But the tone of that thought changed every time he thought it, until he wasn't pissed off at all. He was almost laughing.

And he worried maybe he'd come on a bit strong and scared the guy with all his pretend domination, but look at Shaggy now: wearing Comet's jeans down around one ankle; mussed hair like dark fire, curled tips of it hanging just over the reinforced collar of his jacket— Comet's jacket—the contrast of the blue armor and the soft lily-pink ass beneath it so stark. And look at Comet's cock: there were still a couple centimeters of it he could see, but the other fifteen were buried in the guy—hell, maybe twenty as hard as Comet was; so hard it felt like his cock would split open. And when he pulled out, the orange hairs of Shaggy's ass stuck to Comet's cock by the spit that lubed him up.

And Shaggy wasn't fighting him anymore, no matter what kind of oh-god-help-me noises he was making. His back was bowed and his ass was high, and he was pushing and wriggling down on Comet every bit as much as Comet was shoving into him.

Goddamn but his ass was as tight as a flea's.

Comet fucked the way he liked to fuck: hard and solid, needing every whimper Shaggy gave him, needing to be deeper in him, deeper than he could ever possibly be. And if he hurt Shaggy a bit, well Shaggy deserved some of it, didn't he? Because Shaggy was a little arrogant prick too. And he needed a lesson taught. And Comet hammered him hard enough to make the bike wobble and make Shaggy's breath burst out in puffs of "oh" and "ah" and hisses.

Whatever the lesson was supposed to be, Comet taught it.

And there were so many things he wanted to do to him. And he wanted to know the noises Shaggy would make if he did this or that or this other, and he wanted to know what would make Shaggy come, and so sometimes he held Shaggy's chained-up hands. And he slapped his ass sometimes, and pulled his hair sometimes, and bit the lobe of his ear sometimes, and kissed him sometimes. He wanted to know everything about how Shaggy's body worked. He threw his head back and grinned up at the blue sky and prayed some kind of thank you, though to who, he didn't know. And looked down again and there was *his* bike and *his* jeans and *his* jacket, and there was this guy that *wasn't* his and would always be something wild, and Comet would always be chasing him and trying to tie him down. And the thought of endless pursuit and capture, what else could he ever want?

And the same errant thought came to him as it always had before because Comet never went long without thinking of his team. They were his Greek chorus: *You fucked an internationally wanted thief on the back of your bike, what the hell were you thinking?*

What the hell he was thinking was this: *You knew in that alley that cyborg would hurt you and you let her hack you anyway just so you could hack her back. You broke out of those cuffs at my apartment and then apologized for it like you'd been rude. You told me I scared you and it made me feel like shit. You took a bullet to the arm and were proud of it. You're scared of motorcycles, but you piloted one anyway. You came back for me when I was down and found me when I was lost.* And he said to the Reindeer: *What else could I have done?*

When everything was coming apart, what else were you supposed to do but fall in love?

All the crazy mods in his rewired body tightened and fired, all the made-for-fucking biology Duke had specced into him because Duke liked to watch Comet reduced to helplessness when he came. His body spasmed and shuddered and ejected his very soul out of him, twenty-one grams of come, twenty-one milliliters if anyone was measuring, and that was a whole lot of come. Comet shot it into Shaggy, stream after stream after stream of it.

The first time he'd come with this brand-new cock jacking off in that hospital bed with Duke watching, it had scared the hell out of him. He'd thought something had broken in his hot-wired body, that they'd hooked something together wrong and it was shutting down. The world had gone all dim, and he couldn't see or smell or taste anything. Same as now.

Comet came back to his senses one at a time. He tasted the sweat and dirt on Shaggy's neck where he kissed him. He smelled asphalt and dust and pungent sweat. He heard the sharp prayer-like breaths Shaggy took. He felt balanced precariously: bent over Shaggy, bent over the bike on its kickstand.

Comet pulled Shaggy standing. Shaggy couldn't stand, legs numb and cramped, so Comet wrapped his arm tight around his chest like some kind of wrestling hold and held him up. And he jacked him off. Shaggy's head fell back, eyes on the sky just as Comet's had been, soft hair against Comet's cheek. He gasped short breaths and fucked himself on Comet's cock still in him until Comet felt Shaggy's cuffed hands clench tight and felt the wetness pour over his own hand and saw Shaggy's white spatter his bike and drip thickly from one piece of flame-colored plastic to the next piece of carbon steel, hanging in long sun-sparkling threads. He stroked the last bit of Shaggy's jizz out of him until Shaggy winced.

"I came on your bike again."

"Some people never learn. Next time you do that, you're gonna lick it up."

He laid Shaggy down in the regrown druid-grass. It was thick and warm and took the edge off the gravel and hard earth beneath them like the druids had known they'd fuck here and had made the grass just for them.

And everything smelled alive, sweet and fragrant with flax and aster and the clean-bleach scent of their come. They kissed and held each other a long time and they didn't talk because they didn't know how to yet, so Comet slid into him again and made love to him this time, slow like it was meant to be done, and the sun went red and bloomed on the horizon as giant and shimmering as Comet felt.

Click. Comet looked down at his hand. Shaggy had cuffed the two of them together.

"How'd you do that?"

"It's just a counter and a transmitter. I can do that without the chip. It's just the range that's—"

Comet shushed him with a kiss. "Little smart-ass." And they kissed again, and Comet held his chin and looked into his eyes. "I don't know anything about you."

"No." And Shaggy choked on the word so it wasn't a word as much as a sound.

"What?" Comet laughed. "You afraid I'm gonna find something I don't like? Afraid I'm gonna leave you?"

And Comet's stomach went all vertigo with the sad look Shaggy gave him, because he knew something bad was about to happen, bad like he'd known when he'd stepped off that plane and Jason hadn't been there.

"No," Shaggy said. "I'm the one who's leaving."

Shaggy told Comet about High Castle, 3djinn, BangBang, Critter, and C#Minor. He told him how BangBang had tried to kill him. He told him how he understood all of it now—his physical body wasn't a liability just to 3djinn, but to everyone he ever loved—and when he got back to Greentown, he was going to deep sleep in High Castle.

He said "High Castle" like it was some magical place, like Disney World or Jurassic Park, but Comet knew it was some kind of body bank, a pit a kilometer underground, some long-lost nuclear-missile vault, converted over, the kind of place where stim addicts "lived," if you could call it that.

"No," Comet said with the flat kind of tone he used with the Reindeer when they were giving him flack. "No."

That tone didn't work with Shaggy. "You got net access. So nothing changes, right? You just close your eyes and there we are together. And there's good programs now, really good simulations, and you won't know the difference, and I can make myself whatever you want—"

"I want what you are."

"We can have sex on a beach. We can have dinner in Paris. We can do whatever we want. We can write it so you won't even know the difference. You can't even tell where real lets off and the network starts—that's how good we can make it."

"And when I'm deployed and blacknetted? Or we're in fucking Nevada?"

"I'll send a recorded VI of myself. You can sim it whenever you want!"

"A fucking recording? A fucking *recording*?"

"There's no difference!"

"What about now? What about all this we've done over the last day? You gonna sim all that too? You know why we're fucking right now? Because you were next to me, you were with me through all of that . . . that shit we drove through! Not some goddamn recording. None of this would ever have happened if you hadn't been really here. If you could have just logged out whenever you wanted, if I hadn't worried about you getting hurt, or you hadn't worried about me, or either of us hadn't worried about Jason or Dante . . ." Comet kissed him. He kissed him again and again.

And between kisses he said, "After the druid's hole, we were on the ground and Urushiol and Firelight were arguing over us and you held my hand, but it was only a sim, so I took yours for real. Are you going to tell me it was the same thing?"

Shaggy shook his head sad and slow. "But what else am I supposed to do? They'll kill me, Comet, people like Valentine. And people like Dante will get hurt. And you can't protect me."

Comet started to argue.

"Stop. You can't. You know you can't."

"I'll think of something."

And Comet held him, and all night they made love until they couldn't anymore and even when Comet slept, his mind churned, *Think of something.*

And when the sun came up, and they lay there bleary and uncomfortable because out in the open air on the ground is a shitty place to sleep, Comet said, "Maybe I can't protect you, but Duke can."

CHAPTER FIFTEEN

Two days later, Buzz met them at 501 Main in Greentown. They sat at Duke's corner booth: BangBang (with Critter), Buzz and Comet (sitting far closer than the last time they'd been here together), Duke, and finally Prancer. Prancer was tall, African descent, skin black as it got without mods. She was reed thin like a Spacer. She had cheekbones like knives. Buzz thought she looked like Janeé Awolowo when she'd shaved her head for *Raise High Running*.

BangBang didn't sit on the booth seat with the rest. He sat on a chair at the open arc of the table. Critter was a chinchilla this time. It curled in BangBang's pocket. It was all a complicated illusion. BangBang and Critter were invisible to Duke and Prancer. Buzz could see and hear them, and via Buzz, Comet could too. Prancer was probably skilled enough to know some presence was there, but couldn't quite pin it down.

Duke sized up Buzz the way cannibals picked their dinner, and under Duke's lightning-bolt gaze, Buzz fidgeted so bad he thought he'd bust. Comet touched him gently through their private space. He calmed a little. His vibrating leg went still. Comet sent, —*You're sure about this?*

—*Sure. It ain't like we're getting married.* It wasn't like they were getting married, not at all. It was worse than that, so much worse.

Comet kept that simulated pressure on Buzz's shoulder, and Buzz knew Comet had been right, and this touch here would never be the same as Comet's real touch on him. A sensation was never simply a sensation, because all the firings of the brain and all the wash of chemicals and all the memories of every other touch you ever had gave that touch meaning. When it came down to it, a touch was like a glamour, wasn't it? You could try to re-create it, but the deeply embedded essence of what it was—every touch the culmination of all your life's experience—that was always missing from a sim. A sim was always just fucking. And Comet's simulated touches would never, ever be enough.

This had to work.

Buzz sent Comet a sober thumbs-up. —*Let's do it.*

Duke said, "Comet, why's this guy sitting at my table and not dead or in jail?"

"I want him on Reindeer Squad."

There was a moment of quiet that wasn't quiet at all. The networks surrounding BangBang and Critter went wild. Prancer's reaction was more delicate. The elaborate webbing surrounding her, connecting her to agencies worldwide snapped taut and held itself that way, awaiting Duke's command.

—*You're defecting,* BangBang sent.

—*No,* Buzz sent.

"He wants to defect," Duke said, unable to hear BangBang's or Buzz's response.

"No," Comet said.

—*You think they can protect you from us?*

—*No, BangBang, just listen.*

"He wants my protection against 3djinn. He's crazy."

"No, he doesn't. Duke, please listen."

BangBang sent, —*You broke a contract when you stole the Blue Unicorn, Buzz. And you put us all at risk with your adventuring. And now you're selling data. What the hell is wrong with you?*

—*If I were selling data, I sure as hell wouldn't have invited you along to watch.*

Duke said, "What data do I get?"

"You don't get any data!" Buzz said.

Comet said, "You get the best hacker on the planet, that's what you get."

"Hey, sitting right here," Prancer said.

"He's exaggerating," Buzz said to Prancer.

—*This is about him, isn't it?* BangBang nodded at Comet.

—*Yes,* Buzz sent.

—We gave you everything, and you choose him over us.

—He didn't try to kill me!

—You betrayed us first when you opened yourself up to Valentine!

Buzz pointed at Critter. *—Is that your little squirrel feeding you that line of bullshit?*

"Burn signal detected," Prancer said calmly.

Buzz had known this was coming. On that motorcycle ride back to Greentown, he and Comet had carefully thought through every scenario they could, and all of them came down to this: 3djinn would see Buzz's desire to leave as nothing less than a betrayal. They would hire assassins. They'd lock him out of every system, blacklist him from every community, turn him into a hunted pariah. They'd make the Electric Dragon Triad's pursuit of Buzz, which had ended with dozens dead and a druid's lodge destroyed, look like amateur night. And the only way to mitigate that was to convince them he wasn't selling data, and any effort to ruin him would be a useless expenditure of resources.

There were systems in the networks that Buzz had been tied to for so long they'd become part of the background noise of his mind. Databases he accessed daily, data-mining applications that fed his VIs, Indigo and Ultraviolet invite-only shared spaces that always hummed like the conversation from two tables over. Those things went silent as 3djinns's burn signal cut him off. It was like having parts of his mind removed.

"Wow," Prancer said. Because what it would look like to Prancer was the entire network in rebellion. News of Buzz's "defection" shot everywhere, and suddenly 3djinn's fortunes down-shifted. Alliances between network polities formed and broke in moments. Prancer's unfocused eyes focused for just a moment on Buzz, as if reassessing.

One second passed.

Buzz Howdy appeared on the Interpol most wanted, and Pacifica, CTexas, Confederation, Carib, and New England Bureaus of Investigation.

"Duke?" Prancer said, because Buzz's value was decreasing by the nanosecond.

And Buzz wanted to fight what 3djinn was doing, but he and Comet had talked about this too. If he fought 3djinn, they'd take it as evidence he was stealing from them. And if he sat here and did nothing, it would force Duke's hand, right? Right? That was the plan.

It sure as hell didn't look like their plan was working.

"Give me something," Duke said to Buzz.

"No."

"Then let him burn," Duke told Prancer.

Prancer looked at Comet, as if Comet had the final say. Comet didn't.

Another second ticked past. Small wars broke out in the network. Buzz started bouncing his leg again, and this time Comet's touch couldn't stop him.

A bounty appeared for him on an Ultraviolet site. It raced up to 200 million before Buzz was cut off from the site entirely.

"Duke . . ." Prancer said.

Duke glared at Comet. It was a strange kind of permission. Comet said, "Do it."

Prancer transmitted a simple message to a whole lot of power brokers worldwide: *Buzz Howdy belongs to Duke Mason.*

And all those power brokers stopped their little wars to reassess. 3djinn stopped their attacks. Buzz's name disappeared from Bureau of Investigation lists. BangBang gave Buzz a look somewhere between hurt and pissed off. Critter chittered at him. BangBang sent, *—Critter says to tell you, "Don't think this is over."* And then he and the chinchilla disappeared.

Buzz slumped in his seat and sighed. The plan had worked. He was free. More or less. He was free enough. *—Next time, let's just get married.*

Shaggy dissolved from the shared space they'd built for the meeting. Prancer dropped the space entirely and Comet couldn't even tell. The table was exactly the same: same empties, same rings of condensation, Comet, Duke, and Prancer in exactly the same places.

"So where is my new employee?" Duke said.

Comet only shrugged. He took a deep, long drink from his beer that had gone warm a long time ago.

Duke said, "That boy's a bad influence on you."

You don't know the half of it, Comet thought. "I didn't feel like I had a choice."

"Probably you didn't." Duke sighed, chest heaving out ridiculously large. He looked to the ceiling and said, "It's always the ones you love most that hurt you the worst."

Comet rolled his eyes at the melodrama, but he was glad for it because that meant things were okay between them. "And Jason? I mean JT?"

Duke had never said one word about Jason's confession of who he was. Jason, Dante, and Austin had never come back to Greentown. The three of them had fallen off the map.

"Don't push me, Comet."

"Yes, sir."

Comet finished his beer and said thanks to Prancer. Prancer was barely paying attention, all her thoughts likely in the net as she tried to assess the full magnitude of what they'd just done.

"Where are you going?" Duke said as Comet slid from the booth.

"I'm going to find my boyfriend before he gets himself into trouble."

EPILOGUE

The table at 501 Main, Duke, Prancer, and the guy Buzz loved dissolved away. Buzz could have kept the link with Comet. He didn't. That link made Comet feel present in an uncanny way, like he was always standing behind Buzz, always about to brush Buzz's hair from his eyes the way Comet did. It was too much.

JT, Austin, and Dante all sat at the dining table, everyone's eyes on him.

They'd broken into some superstar athlete's house overlooking Buena Vista Park. Buzz had complained it was a terrible hideout: too out-in-the-open, too many nosy neighbors willing to call the cops. Austin said he'd handle it, and so far he had. The mansion had a walk-in shower as big as a Chrysler with six shower heads and two Jacuzzis, one hot and one cold. It had six bedrooms with canopy beds, and all those beds did was make Buzz think of Comet and zip ties.

They hadn't fucked nearly as much as each other had wanted. Comet's wounds finally caught up to him, and his body had gone into some kind of repair mode. He'd slept a lot (and Buzz had to pilot the bike) and ate everything (and they stopped for food in every other town) and ran a terrifying fever Comet said was perfectly normal (and Comet's come had gone extra-warm and tasted like apple pie, which had been too strange to enjoy as much as he should have). And then Buzz had gone to meet with JT, Austin, and Dante. Comet had gone back to Duke.

Buzz glanced around the table, sighed, and prepared himself for the inevitable mocking. Comet was getting payback for this one.

"Codename: Vixen."

Dante wasn't sure she trusted this guy. He was banging Comet, after all. She'd met Comet when she'd tried to steal JT's truck. She'd gotten it barely a meter down the road when the guy dragged her out of the cab by her hair, clocked her in the jaw, and broke her tusk. He'd never said he was sorry, not even after she'd started her apprenticeship with JT. In fact, he'd become even more of a jerk. And this guy Buzz, well he didn't seem so bad, but he was dating Comet, so if nothing else, it meant he had shitty taste in men.

Since coming out of her coma (and refusing to acknowledge that elf had anything to do with it), she'd been doing okay. She had a kickass cane with a knotted top some druid had shaped to look creepy, and she was thinking she'd carry it around even when she didn't need it anymore. But she'd had migraines and crazy dreams too. Dreams of a unicorn being slaughtered by elves. Those were wearing her down.

Buzz said he knew what was causing those dreams, and he could fix it.

He'd set up a small holo-projector in the middle of the table and fired up a virtual copy of the computer that ran JT's 3-D printer back in Greentown. A miniature pickup truck with oversized wheels appeared. It was Dante's journeyman project. JT's mouth twitched when he saw it. It was close enough to a smile that Dante felt sure everyone could see her glow.

The truck door opened and a woman stepped out. She was the Blue Unicorn, the AI fragment JT, Austin, and Buzz had rescued from the Electric Dragon Triad. She said, "Help me, Dante Riggs. You're my only hope."

Dante remembered none of this. Buzz said it was normal to not remember events right before a trauma. Buzz wasn't a doctor, so how the fuck did he know what was normal or not?

The projection went static and looped and started again. Buzz dimmed the sound.

"When we set the Blue Unicorn free, we all figured we'd seen the last of it. I had added some tracking code—"

"You did what?" Austin said, annoyed.

"Oh relax. Did you honestly think I *wasn't* going to track her? Anyway, it didn't work. I don't know where she went. What I knew was that four hours later she came back. She slipped through JT's firewall using a vulnerability in the 1Night social net."

JT glared at Dante. Dante ignored him. She had needs after all.

"And then this happened." And Buzz played the loop again.

"Help me, Dante Riggs . . ." And at the end of the recording, Buzz paused it again.

"And then Valentine attacked, hitting the network first. The Blue Unicorn knew JT's defenses wouldn't hold, so it encrypted its message and hid the rest of the recording in Dante's head."

"And then dropped her into a coma?" JT said.

"I don't think so. I think Dante stayed in the network too long, and Valentine burned her."

"This recording, is that what's causing my headaches and the dreams?"

Buzz shrugged. "JT's network is a mess, and I'm not a forensics expert, but it makes sense. It's the best I've got, sorry."

"So all I gotta do is unlock the rest of the message and play it?"

"Yep."

"But I don't have a recording."

"Yeah, you do," Buzz said, "You just don't know it. You're having dreams of the unicorn. Most likely the recording was something repeating in your head while you were unconscious."

"Trucks," Austin said. "She was driving her truck."

"We were going West. Following the elves." She wouldn't look at Austin.

"Copy over your project file, the one with the truck, and run it. I'm pretty sure—"

But she'd been one step ahead of him.

The truck rotated lazily, huge and tiny on its projection disk. Its door opened. The Blue Unicorn stepped down. Butterflies swirled around her afro. Her long elven ears poked from frizzy hair.

"Help me, Dante Riggs. You're my only hope. This fragment has been named the Blue Unicorn. This fragment is one of hundreds shaved from the parent mind as proof of her existence, all seeking JT and Austin. This fragment is the only one to ever have returned to the parent. The others have been lost. This fragment believes you are a conduit to JT. Your soul matches his. The parent mind is sorry to drag you into this. The parent mind suggests you choose better passwords. The parent mind hopes you do not die."

The tiny truck and its tiny woman disappeared, and the projector erupted with floor plans, electrical and HVAC plans, network diagrams, personnel and security rosters, and all the weird ephemera of the bleakest sorcery. It was Alcatraz Island.

A voice overrode the images. It wasn't quite the same as the Unicorn's voice. This one was natural, more human. The voice gave Dante chills. It was so familiar, and yet she'd never heard it before.

"JT? Austin? I'm trapped. I can't get out of here. Please help me. I've got no one else to turn to. You don't know me. My name is Roan."

THE GLAMOUR THIEVES

★ "Swoonworthy."
—*Publishers Weekly,*
Starred Review

BLUE UNICORN 🦄 BOOK ONE

DON ALLMON

Dear Reader,

Thank you for reading Don Allmon's *Apocalypse Alley*!

We know your time is precious and you have many, many entertainment options, so it means a lot that you've chosen to spend your time reading. We really hope you enjoyed it.

We'd be honored if you'd consider posting a review—good or bad—on sites like **Amazon, Barnes & Noble, Kobo, Goodreads, Twitter, Facebook, Tumblr,** and your blog or website. We'd also be honored if you told your friends and family about this book. Word of mouth is a book's lifeblood!

For more information on upcoming releases, author interviews, blog tours, contests, giveaways, and more, please sign up for our weekly, spam-free newsletter and visit us around the web:

Newsletter: tinyurl.com/RiptideSignup
Twitter: twitter.com/RiptideBooks
Facebook: facebook.com/RiptidePublishing
Goodreads: tinyurl.com/RiptideOnGoodreads
Tumblr: riptidepublishing.tumblr.com

Thank you so much for Reading the Rainbow!

RiptidePublishing.com

ACKNOWLEDGMENTS

Eternal thanks to my editor, Sarah Lyons, for her invaluable help with a major revision that saved the story. Many thanks to my agent, Sara Megibow, for her boundless and contagious optimism. To Shawn, whose martial arts DVDs I have finally returned. And to Travis, who continues to endure my writerly angst with saintlike patience and grace.

ALSO BY DON ALLMON

Blue Unicorn series
The Glamour Thieves
The Burning Magus (coming soon)

ABOUT THE AUTHOR

In his night job, Don Allmon writes science fiction, fantasy, and romance. In his day job, he's an IT drone. He holds a master of arts in English literature from the University of Kansas and wrote his thesis on the influence of royal hunting culture on medieval werewolf stories. He's a fan of role-playing games, both video and tabletop. He has lived all over from New York to San Francisco, but currently lives on the prairies of Kansas with many animals.

Connect with Don:

Website: www.donallmon.com

Twitter: @dallmon

Pinterest: pinterest.com/donallmon

Enjoy more stories like
Apocalypse Alley
at RiptidePublishing.com!

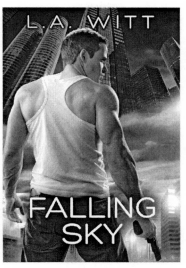
Earn Bonus Bucks!

Earn 1 Bonus Buck for each dollar you spend. Find out how at
RiptidePublishing.com/news/bonus-bucks.

Win Free Ebooks for a Year!

Pre-order coming soon titles directly through our site and you'll
receive one entry into a drawing for a chance to win free books for
a year! Get the details at RiptidePublishing.com/contests.

CPSIA information can be obtained
at www.ICGtesting.com
Printed in the USA
LVOW12s1621130318
569702LV00004B/690/P